The Cattle-Raid of Cualnge

Unknown

Contents

THE CATTLE-RAID
OF CUALNGE

BY

Unknown

INTRODUCTION

The Cattle-Raid of Cualnge [Note: Pronounce **Cooley**] is the chief story belonging to the heroic cycle of Ulster, which had its centre in the deeds of the Ulster king, Conchobar Mac Nessa, and his nephew and chief warrior, Cuchulainn Mac Sualtaim. Tradition places their date at the beginning of the Christian era.

The events leading up to this tale, the most famous of Irish mythical stories, may be shortly summarised here from the Book of Leinster introduction to the *Tain*, and from the other tales belonging to the Ulster cycle.

It is elsewhere narrated that the Dun Bull of Cualnge, for whose sake Ailill and Medb [Note: Pronounce **Maive**.], the king and queen of Connaught, undertook this expedition, was one of two bulls in whom two rival swineherds, belonging to the supernatural race known as the people of the *Sid*, or fairy-mounds, were reincarnated, after passing through various other forms. The other bull, Findbennach, the White-horned, was in the herd of Medb at Cruachan Ai, the Connaught capital, but left it to join Ailill's herd. This caused Ailill's possessions to exceed Medb's, and to equalise matters she determined to secure the great Dun Bull, who alone equalled the White-horned. An embassy to the owner of the Dun Bull failed, and Ailill and Medb therefore began preparations for an invasion of Ulster, in which province (then ruled by Conchobar Mac Nessa) Cualnge was situated. A number of smaller *Tana*, or cattle-raids, prefatory to the great *Tain Bo Cuailnge*, relate some of their efforts to procure allies and provisions.

Medb chose for the expedition the time when Conchobar and all the warriors of Ulster, except Cuchulainn and Sualtaim, were at their capital, Emain Macha, in a sickness which fell on them periodically, making them powerless for action; another story relates the cause of this sickness, the effect of a curse laid on them by a fairy woman. Ulster was therefore defended only by the seventeen-year-old Cuchulainn, for Sualtaim's appearance is only spasmodic. Cuchulainn (Culann's Hound) was the son of Dechtire, the king's sister, his father being, in different accounts, either Sualtaim, an Ulster warrior; Lug Mac Ethlend, one of the divine heroes from the *Sid*, or fairy-mound; or Conchobar himself. The two former both appear as Cuchulainn's father in the present narrative. Cuchulainn is accompanied, throughout the adventures here told, by his charioteer, Loeg Mac Riangabra.

In Medb's force were several Ulster heroes, including Cormac Condlongas, son of Conchobar, Conall Cernach, Dubthach Doeltenga, Fiacha Mac Firfebe, and Fergus Mac Roich. These were exiled from Ulster through a bitter quarrel with Conchobar, who had caused the betrayal and murder of the sons of Uisnech, when they had come to Ulster under the sworn protection of Fergus, as told in the *Exile of the Sons of Uisnech*. [Note: 1 Text in Windisch and Stokes's *Irische Texte*; English translation in Miss Hull's *Cuchullin Saga*.] The Ulster mischief-maker, Bricriu of the Poison-tongue, was also with the Connaught army. Though fighting for Connaught, the exiles have a friendly feeling for their former comrades, and a keen jealousy for the credit of Ulster. There is a constant interchange of courtesies between them and their old pupil, Cuchulainn, whom they do not scruple to exhort to fresh efforts for Ulster's honour. An equally half-hearted warrior is Lugaid Mac Nois, king of Munster, who was bound in friendship to the Ulstermen.

Other characters who play an important part in the story are Findabair, daughter of Ailill and Medb, who is held out as a bribe to various heroes to induce them to fight Cuchulainn, and is on one occasion offered to the latter in fraud on condition that he will give up his opposition to the host; and the war-goddess, variously styled the Nemain, the Badb (scald-crow), and the Morrigan (great queen), who takes part against Cuchulainn in one of his chief fights. Findabair is the bait which induces several old comrades of Cuchulainn's, who had been his fellow-pupils under the sorceress Scathach, to fight him in single combat.

The tale may be divided into:--

1. Introduction: Fedelm's prophecy.

2. Cuchulainn's first feats against the host, and the several *geis*, or taboos, which he lays on them.

3. The narration of Cuchulainn's boyish deeds, by the Ulster exiles to the Con-

naught host.

4. Cuchulainn's harassing of the host.

5. The bargain and series of single combats, interrupted by breaches of the agreement on the part of Connaught.

6. The visit of Lug Mac Ethlend.

7. The fight with Fer Diad.

8. The end: the muster of the Ulstermen.

The MSS.

The *Tain Bo Cuailnge* survives, in whole or in part, in a considerable number of MSS., most of which are, however, late. The most important are three in number:--

(1) Leabhar na h-Uidhri (LU), 'The Book of the Dun Cow,' a MS. dating from about 1100. The version here given is an old one, though with some late additions, in later language. The chief of these are the piece coming between the death of the herd Forgemen and the fight with Cur Mac Dalath (including Cuchulainn's meeting with Findabair, and the 'womanfight' of Rochad), and the whole of what follows the Healing of the Morrigan. The tale is, like others in this MS., unfinished, the MS. being imperfect.

(2) The Yellow Book of Lecan (YBL), a late fourteenth-century MS. The *Tain* in this is substantially the same as in LU. The beginning is missing, but the end is given. Some of the late additions of LU are not found here; and YBL, late as it is, often gives an older and better text than the earlier MS.

(3) The Book of Leinster (LL), before 1160. The *Tain* here is longer, fuller, and later in both style and language than in LU or YBL. It is essentially a literary attempt to give a complete and consistent narrative, and is much less interesting than the older LU-YBL recension.

In the present version, I have collated LU, as far as it goes, with YBL, adding from the latter the concluding parts of the story, from the Fight with Fer Diad to the end. After the Fight with Fer Diad, YBL breaks off abruptly, leaving nearly a page blank; then follow several pages containing lists, alternative versions of some episodes given in LU (Rochad's Woman-fight, the Warning to Conchobar), and one or two episodes which are narrated in LL. I omit about one page, where the narrative is broken and confused.

The pages which follow the Healing of the Morrigan in LU are altogether different in style from the rest of the story as told in LU, and are out of keeping with its simplicity. This whole portion is in the later manner of LL, with which, for the most part, it is in verbal agreement. Further, it is in part repetition of material already given (i.e. the coming of the boy-host of Ulster, and Cuchulainn's displaying himself to the Connaught troops).

COMPARISON OF THE VERSIONS

A German translation of the Leinster text of the **Tain Bo Cuailnge** will soon be accessible to all in Dr. Windisch's promised edition of the text. It is therefore unnecessary to compare the two versions in detail. Some of the main differences may be pointed out, however.

Of our three copies none is the direct ancestor of any other. LU and YBL are from a common source, though the latter MS. is from an older copy; LL is independent. The two types differ entirely in aim and method. The writers of LU and YBL aimed at accuracy; the Leinster man, at presenting an intelligible version. Hence, where the two former reproduce obscurities and corruptions, the latter omits, paraphrases, or expands. The unfortunate result is that LL rarely, if ever, helps to clear up textual obscurities in the older copy.

On the other hand, it offers explanations of certain episodes not clearly stated in LU. Thus, for example, where LU, in the story of the sons of Nechta Scene, simply mentions 'the withe that was on the pillar,' LL explains that the withe had been placed there by the sons of Nechta Scene (as Cuchulainn placed a similar with in the path of the Connaught host), with an ogam inscription forbidding any to pass without combat; hence its removal was an insult and a breach of *geis*. Again, the various embassies to Cuchulainn, and the terms made with him (that he should not harass the host if he were supplied daily with food, and with a champion to meet him in single combat), are more clearly described in LL.

Some of the episodes given in LU are not told in the Leinster version. Of the boyish deeds of Cuchulainn, LL tells only three: his first appearance at Emain (told by Fergus), Culann's feast (by Cormac), and the feats following Cuchulainn's taking of arms (by Fiacha). In the main narrative, the chief episodes omitted in LL are the fight with Fraech, the Fergus and Medb episode, and the meeting of Findabair and Cuchulainn. The meeting with the Morrigan is missing, owing to the loss of a leaf. Other episodes are differently placed in LL: e.g. the Rochad story (an entirely different account), the fight of Amairgen and Curoi with stones, and the warning to Conchobar, all follow the fight with Fer Diad.

A peculiarity of the LU-YBL version is the number of passages which it has in common with the ***Dinnsenchas***, an eleventh-century compilation of place-legends. The existing collections of ***Dinnsenchas*** contain over fifty entries derived from the ***Tain*** cycle, some corresponding with, others differing from those in LU.

This version has also embodied a considerable number of glosses in the text. As many of these are common to LU and YBL, they must go back to the common original, which must therefore have been a harmony of previously existing versions, since many of these passages give variants of incidents.

AGE OF THE VERSIONS

There is no doubt that the version here translated is a very old one. The language in LU is almost uniformly Middle Irish, not more than a century earlier than the date of the MS.; thus it shows the post-thetic *he*, *iat*, etc. as object, the adverb with *co*, the confusion of *ar* and *for*, the extension of the *b*-future, etc. But YBL preserves forms as old as the Glosses:--

(1) The correct use of the infixed relative, e.g. ***rombith***, 'with which he struck.' (LU, ***robith***, 58a, 45.)

(2) The infixed accusative pronoun, e.g. ***nachndiusced***, 'that he should not wake him.' (LU, ***nach diusced***, 62a, 30.)

(3) ***no*** with a secondary tense, e.g. ***nolinad***, 'he used to fill.' (LU, ***rolinad***, 60b, 6.)

(4) Very frequently YBL keeps the right aspirated or non-aspirated consonant, where LU shows a general confusion, etc.

LL has no very archaic forms, though it cultivates a pseudo-archaic style; and it is unlikely that the Leinster version goes back much earlier than 1050. The latter part of the LU *Tain* shows that a version of the Leinster type was known to the compiler. The style of this part, with its piling-up of epithets, is that of eleventh-century narrative, as exemplified in texts like the **Cath Ruis na Rig** and the **Cogadh Gaidhil**; long strings of alliterative epithets, introduced for sound rather than sense, are characteristic of the period. The descriptions of chariots and horses in the Fer Diad episode in YBL are similar, and evidently belong to the same rescension.

The inferences from the facts noted in the foregoing sections may be stated as follows: A version of the *Tain* goes back to the early eighth, or seventh century, and is preserved under the YBL text; an opinion based on linguistic evidence, but coinciding with the tradition which ascribes the 'Recovery of the *Tain*' to Senchan Torpeist, a bard of the later seventh century. This version continued to be copied down to the eleventh century, gradually changing as the language changed. Meanwhile, varying accounts of parts of the story came into existence, and some time in the eleventh century a new redaction was made, the oldest representative of which is the LL text. Parts of this were embodied in or added to the older version; hence the interpolations in LU.

THE FER DIAD EPISODE

There is much difference between the two versions of this episode. In YBL, the introductory portion is long and full, the actual fight very short, while in LL the fight is long-drawn-out, and much more stress is laid on the pathetic aspect of the situation. Hence it is generally assumed that LL preserves an old version of the episode, and that the scribe of the Yellow Book has compressed the latter part. It is not, however, usual, in primitive story-telling, to linger over scenes of pathos. Such lingering is, like the painted tears of late Italian masters, invariably a sign of decadence. It is one of the marks of romance, which recognises tragedy only when it is voluble, and prodigal of lamentation. The older version of the *Tain* is throughout singularly free from pathos of the feebler sort; the humorous side is always uppermost, and the tragic suggestions interwoven with it.

But it is still a matter of question whether the whole Fer Diad episode may not be late. Professor Zimmer thinks it is; but even the greatest scholar, with a theory to prove, is not quite free. It will of course be noticed, on this side, that the chief motives of the Fer Diad episode all appear previously in other episodes (e.g. the fights with Ferbaeth and with Loch). Further, the account even in YBL is not marked by old linguistic forms as are other parts of the tale, while much of it is in the bombastic descriptive style of LL. In the condition in which we have the tale, however, this adventure is treated as the climax of the story. Its motive is to remove Cuchulainn from the field, in order to give the rest of Ulster a chance. But in the account of the final great fight in YBL, Cuchulainn's absence is said to be due to his having been wounded in a combat against odds (***crechtnugud i n-ecomlund***). Considering, therefore, that even in YBL the Fer Diad episode is late in language, it seems possible that it may have replaced some earlier account in which Cuchulainn was so severely wounded that he was obliged to retire from the field.

PREVIOUS WORK ON THE '*TAIN*'

Up to the present time the *Tain* has never been either printed or translated, though the LU version has been for thirty years easily accessible in facsimile. Dr. Windisch's promised edition will shortly be out, containing the LL and LU texts, with a German translation of the former. The most useful piece of work done hitherto for the *Tain* is the analysis by Professor Zimmer of the LU text (conclusion from the Book of Leinster), in the fifth of his Keltische Studien (Zeitschrift fuer vergl. Sprachforschung, xxviii.). Another analysis of the story, by Mr. S. H. O'Grady, appeared in Miss Eleanor Hull's *The Cuchullin Saga*; it is based on a late paper MS. in the British Museum, giving substantially the same version as LL. This work contains also a map of ancient Ireland, showing the route of the Connaught forces; but a careful working-out of the topography of the *Tain* is much needed, many names being still unidentified. Several of the small introductory *Tana* have been published in Windisch and Stokes's *Irische Texte*; and separate episodes from the great *Tain* have been printed and translated from time to time. The Fight with Fer Diad (LL) was printed with translation by O'Curry in the *Manners and Customs of the Ancient Irish*. The story of the Two Swineherds, with their successive reincarnations until they became the Dun Bull and the White-horned (an introductory story to the *Tain*), is edited with translation in *Irische Texte*, and Mr. Nutt printed an abridged English version in the *Voyage of Bran*.

The Leinster version seems to have been the favourite with modern workers, probably because it is complete and consistent; possibly its more sentimental style has also served to commend it.

AIM OF THIS TRANSLATION

It is perhaps unnecessary to say that the present version is intended for those who cannot read the tale in the original; it is therefore inadvisable to overload the volume with notes, variant readings, or explanations of the readings adopted, which might repel the readers to whom it is offered.

At the present time, an enthusiasm for Irish literature is not always accompanied by a knowledge of the Irish language. It seems therefore to be the translator's duty, if any true estimate of this literature is to be formed, to keep fairly close to the original, since nothing is to be gained by attributing beauties which it does not possess, while obscuring its true merits, which are not few. For the same reason, while keeping the Irish second person singular in verses and formal speech, I have in ordinary dialogue substituted the pronoun *you*, which suggests the colloquial style of the original better than the obsolete *thou*.

The so-called rhetorics are omitted in translating; they are passages known in Irish as *rosc*, often partly alliterative, but not measured. They are usually meaningless strings of words, with occasional intelligible phrases. In all probability the passages aimed at sound, with only a general suggestion of the drift. Any other omissions are marked where they occur; many obscure words in the long descriptive passages are of necessity left untranslated. In two places I have made slight verbal changes without altering the sense, a liberty which is very rarely necessary in Irish.

Of the headings, those printed in capitals are in the text in the MS.; those italicised are marginal. I have bracketed obvious scribal glosses which have crept into the text. Some of the marginal glosses are translated in the footnotes.

GEOGRAPHICAL NAMES

As a considerable part of the *Tain* is occupied by connecting episodes with place-names, an explanation of some of the commonest elements in these may be of use to those who know no Irish:

Ath=a ford; e.g. Ath Gabla (Ford of the Fork), Ath Traiged (Ford of the Foot), Ath Carpat (Ford of Chariots), Ath Fraich (Fraech's Ford), etc.

Belat=cross-roads; e.g. Belat Alioin.

Bernas=a pass, or gap; e.g. **Bernas Bo Ulad** or **Bernas Bo Cuailnge** (Pass of the Cows of Ulster, or of Cualnge).

Clithar=a shelter; e.g. Clithar Bo Ulad (shelter of the Cows of Ulster).

Cul=a corner; e.g. Cul Airthir (eastern corner).

Dun= a fort; e.g. Dun Sobairche.

Fid=a wood; e.g. Fid Mor Drualle (Great Wood of the Sword-sheath).

Glass=a brook, stream; e.g. Glass Chrau (the stream of Blood), Glass Cruind, Glass Gatlaig (gatt=a withe, laig=a calf).

Glenn=a glen; e.g. Glenn Gatt (Glen of the Withe), Glenn Firbaith (Ferbaeth's Glen), Glenn Gatlaig.

Grellach=a bog; e.g. Grellach Doluid.

Guala=a hill-shoulder; e.g. Gulo Mulchai (Mulcha's shoulder).

Loch=a lake; e.g. Loch Reoin, Loch Echtra.

Mag=a plain; e.g. Mag Ai, Mag Murthemne, Mag Breg, Mag Clochair (cloch=a stone).

Methe, explained as if from meth (death); Methe Togmaill (death of the Squirrel), Methe n-Eoin (death of the Bird).

Reid, gen. Rede=a plain; e.g. Ath Rede Locha (Ford of Locha's Plain).

Sid=a fairy mound; e.g. Sid Fraich (Fraech's Mound).

Sliab=a mountain; e.g. Sliab Fuait.

I need perhaps hardly say that many of the etymologies given in Irish sources are pure invention, stories being often made up to account for the names, the real meaning of which was unknown to the mediaeval story-teller or scribe.

In conclusion, I have to express my most sincere thanks to Professor Strachan, whose pupil I am proud to be. I have had the advantage of his wide knowledge and experience in dealing with many obscurities in the text, and he has also read the proofs. I am indebted also to Mr. E. Gwynn, who has collated at Trinity College, Dublin, a number of passages in the Yellow Book of Lecan, which are illegible or incorrect in the facsimile; and to Dr. Whitley Stokes for notes and suggestions on many obscure words.

LLANDAFF, November 1903.

THIS IS THE CATTLE-RAID OF CUALNGE

A great hosting was brought together by the Connaughtmen, that is, by Ailill and Medb; and they sent to the three other provinces. And messengers were sent by Ailill to the seven sons of Magach: Ailill, Anluan, Mocorb, Cet, En, Bascall, and Doche; a cantred with each of them. And to Cormac Condlongas Mac Conchobair with his three hundred, who was billeted in Connaught. Then they all come to Cruachan Ai.

Now Cormac had three troops which came to Cruachan. The first troop had many-coloured cloaks folded round them; hair like a mantle (?); the tunic falling(?) to the knee, and long(?) shields; and a broad grey spearhead on a slender shaft in the hand of each man.

The second troop wore dark grey cloaks, and tunics with red ornamentation down to their calves, and long hair hanging behind from their heads, and white shields (?), and five-pronged spears were in their hands.

'This is not Cormac yet,' said Medb.

Then comes the third troop; and they wore purple cloaks and hooded tunics with red ornamentation down to their feet, hair smooth to their shoulders, and round shields with engraved edges, and the pillars [Note: i.e. spears as large as pillars, etc.] of a palace in the hand of each man.

'This is Cormac now,' said Medb.

Then the four provinces of Ireland were assembled, till they were in Cruachan Ai. And their poets and their druids did not let them go thence till the end of a fortnight, for waiting for a good omen. Medb said then to her charioteer the day that they set out:

'Every one who parts here to-day from his love or his friend will curse me,' said she, 'for it is I who have gathered this hosting.'

'Wait then,' said the charioteer, 'till I turn the chariot with the sun, and till there come the power of a good omen that we may come back again.'

Then the charioteer turned the chariot, and they set forth. Then they saw a full-grown maiden before them. She had yellow hair, and a cloak of many colours, and a golden pin in it; and a hooded tunic with red embroidery. She wore two shoes with buckles of gold. Her face was narrow below and broad above. Very black were her two eyebrows; her black delicate eyelashes cast a shadow into the middle of her two cheeks. You would think it was with **partaing** [Note: Exact meaning unknown. It is always used in this connection.] her lips were adorned. You would think it was a shower of pearls that was in her mouth, that is, her teeth. She had three tresses: two tresses round her head above, and a tress behind, so that it struck her two thighs behind her. A shuttle [Note: Literally, a beam used for making fringe.] of white metal, with an inlaying of gold, was in her hand. Each of her two eyes had three pupils. The maiden was armed, and there were two black horses to her chariot.

'What is your name?' said Medb to the maiden.

'Fedelm, the prophetess of Connaught, is my name,' said the maiden.

'Whence do you come?' said Medb.

'From Scotland, after learning the art of prophecy,' said the maiden.

'Have you the inspiration(?) which illumines?' [Note: Ir. **imbas forasnai**, the name of a kind of divination.] said Medb.

'Yes, indeed,' said the maiden.

'Look for me how it will be with my hosting,' said Medb.

Then the maiden looked for it; and Medb said: 'O Fedelm the prophetess, how seest thou the host?'

Fedelm answered and said: 'I see very red, I see red.'

'That is not true,' said Medb; 'for Conchobar is in his sickness at Emain and the Ulstermen with him, with all the best [Note: Conjectural; some letters missing. For the Ulster sickness, see Introduction.] of their warriors; and my messengers have come and brought me tidings thence.

'Fedelm the prophetess, how seest thou our host?' said Medb.

'I see red,' said the maiden.

'That is not true,' said Medb; 'for Celtchar Mac Uithichair is in Dun Lethglaise, and a third of the Ulstermen with him; and Fergus, son of Roich, son of Eochaid, is here with us, in exile, and a cantred with him.

'Fedelm the prophetess, how seest thou our host?' said Medb.

'I see very red, I see red,' said the maiden.

'That matters not,' said Medb; 'for there are mutual angers, and quarrels, and wounds very red in every host and in every assembly of a great army. Look again for us then, and tell us the truth.

'Fedelm the prophetess, how seest thou our host?'

'I see very red, I see red,' said Fedelm.

'I see a fair man who will make play

With a number of wounds(?) on his girdle; [Note: Unless this is an allusion to the custom of carrying an enemy's head at the girdle, the meaning is obscure. LL has quite a different reading. The language of this poem is late.]

A hero's flame over his head,
His forehead a meeting-place of victory.

'There are seven gems of a hero of valour
In the middle of his two irises;
There is ---- on his cloak,
He wears a red clasped tunic.

'He has a face that is noble,
Which causes amazement to women.
A young man who is fair of hue
Comes ---- [Note: Five syllables missing.]

'Like is the nature of his valour
To Cuchulainn of Murthemne.
I do not know whose is the Hound
Of Culann, whose fame is the fairest.
But I know that it is thus

That the host is very red from him.

'I see a great man on the plain
He gives battle to the hosts;
Four little swords of feats
There are in each of his two hands.

'Two **Gae-bolga**, he carries them, [Note: The Gae-bolga was a special kind of spear, which only Cuchulainn could use.]

Besides an ivory-hilted sword and spear;
---- [Note: Three syllables missing] he wields to the host;
Different is the deed for which each arm goes from him.

'A man in a battle-girdle (?), of a red cloak,
He puts ---- every plain.
He smites them, over left chariot wheel (?);

The **Riastartha** wounds them. [Note: The Riastartha ('distorted one') was a name given to Cuchulainn because of the contortion, described later, which came over him.]

The form that appeared to me on him hitherto,
I see that his form has been changed.

'He has moved forward to the battle,
If heed is not taken of him it will be treachery.
I think it likely it is he who seeks you:
Cuchulainn Mac Sualtaim.

'He will strike on whole hosts,
He will make dense slaughters of you,
Ye will leave with him many thousands of heads.

The prophetess Fedelm conceals not.

'Blood will rain from warriors' wounds
At the hand of a warrior--'twill be full harm.
He will slay warriors, men will wander
Of the descendants of Deda Mac Sin.
Corpses will be cut off, women will lament
Through the Hound of the Smith that I see.'

The Monday after Samain [Note: Samain, 'summer-end,' about the beginning of November.] they set forth, and this is the way they took: south-east from Cruachan Ai, i.e. by Muicc Cruimb, by Teloch Teora Crich, by Tuaim Mona, by Cul Sibrinne, by Fid, by Bolga, by Coltain, by Glune-gabair, by Mag Trego, by North Tethba, by South Tethba, by Tiarthechta, by Ord, by Slais southwards, by Indiuind, by Carnd, by Ochtrach, by Midi, by Findglassa Assail, by Deilt, by Delind, by Sailig, by Slaibre, by Slechta Selgatar, by Cul Sibrinne, by Ochaind southwards, by Uatu northwards, by Dub, by Comur southwards, by Tromma, by Othromma eastwards, by Slane, by Gortslane, by Druim Licce southwards, by Ath Gabla, by Ard Achad, by Feraind northwards, by Findabair, by Assi southwards, by Druim Salfind, by Druim Cain, by Druim Mac n-Dega, by Eodond Mor, by Eodond Bec, by Methe Togmaill, by Methe Eoin, by Druim Caemtechta, by Scuaip, by Imscuaip, by Cend Ferna, by Baile, by Aile, by Bail Scena, by Dail Scena, by Fertse, by Ross Lochad, by Sale, by Lochmach, by Anmag, by Deind, by Deilt, by Dubglaiss, by Fid Mor, by Colbtha, by Cronn, to Cualnge.

From Findabair Cuailnge, it is thence the hosts of Ireland were divided over the province to seek the Bull. For it is past these places that they came, till they reached Findabair.

(Here ends the title; and the story begins as follows:--

THIS IS THE STORY IN ORDER

When they had come on their first journey from Cruachan as far as Cul Sibrinne, Medb told her charioteer to get ready her nine chariots for her, that she might make a circuit in the camp, to see who disliked and who liked the expedition.

Now his tent was pitched for Ailill, and the furniture was arranged, both beds and coverings. Fergus Mac Roich in his tent was next to Ailill; Cormac Condlongas Mac Conchobair beside him; Conall Cernach by him; Fiacha Mac Fir-Febe, the son of Conchobar's daughter, by him. Medb, daughter of Eochaid Fedlech, was on Ailill's other side; next to her, Findabair, daughter of Ailill and Medb. That was besides servants and attendants.

Medb came, after looking at the host, and she said it were folly for the rest to go on the hosting, if the cantred of the Leinstermen went.

'Why do you blame the men?' said Ailill.

'We do not blame them,' said Medb; 'splendid are the warriors. When the rest were making their huts, they had finished thatching their huts and cooking their food; when the rest were at dinner, they had finished dinner, and their harpers were playing to them. It is folly for them to go,' said Medb; 'it is to their credit the victory of the hosts will be.'

'It is for us they fight,' said Ailill.

'They shall not come with us,' said Medb.

'Let them stay then,' said Ailill.

'They shall not stay,' said Medb. 'They will come on us after we have gone,' said she, 'and seize our land against us.'

'What is to be done to them?' said Ailill; 'will you have them neither stay nor go?'

'To kill them,' said Medb.

'We will not hide that this is a woman's plan,' said Ailill; 'what you say is not good!'

'With this folk,' said Fergus, 'it shall not happen thus (for it is a folk bound by ties to us Ulstermen), unless we are all killed.'

'Even that we could do,' said Medb; 'for I am here with my retinue of two cantreds,' said she, 'and there are the seven Manes, that is, my seven sons, with seven cantreds; their luck can protect them,' (?) said she; 'that is Mane-Mathramail, and Mane-Athramail, and Mane-Morgor, and Mane-Mingor, and Mane-Moepert (and he is Mane-Milscothach), Mane-Andoe, and Mane-who-got-everything: he got the form of his mother and of his father, and the dignity of both.'

'It would not be so,' said Fergus. 'There are seven kings of Munster here, and a cantred with each of them, in friendship with us Ulstermen. I will give battle to you,' said Fergus, 'in the middle of the host in which we are, with these seven cantreds, and with my own cantred, and with the cantred of the Leinstermen. But I will not urge that,' said Fergus, 'we will provide for the warriors otherwise, so that they shall not prevail over the host. Seventeen cantreds for us,' said Fergus, 'that is the number of our army, besides our rabble, and our women (for with each king there is his queen, in Medb's company), and besides our striplings. This is the eighteenth cantred, the cantred of the Leinstermen. Let them be distributed among the rest of the host.'

'I do not care,' said Medb, 'provided they are not gathered as they are.'

Then this was done; the Leinstermen were distributed among the host.

They set out next morning to Moin Choiltrae, where eight score deer fell in with them in one herd. They surrounded them and killed them then; wherever there was a man of the Leinstermen, it was he who got them, except five deer that all the rest of the host got. Then they came to Mag Trego, and stopped there and prepared their food. They say that it is there that Dubthach sang this song:

'Grant what you have not heard hitherto,
Listening to the fight of Dubthach.
A hosting very black is before you,

Against Findbend of the wife of Ailill. [Note: Findbennach, the Whitehorned; i.e. the other of the two bulls in whom the rival swineherds were reincarnated.]

'The man of expeditions will come
Who will defend (?) Murthemne.
Ravens will drink milk of ---- [Note: Some kenning for blood?]
From the friendship of the swineherds.

'The turfy Cronn will resist them; [Note: i.e. the river Cronn. This line is a corruption of a reference which occurs later, in the account of the flooding of the Cronn, as Professor Strachan first pointed out to me.]
He will not let them into Murthemne
Until the work of warriors is over

In Sliab Tuad Ochaine.

'"Quickly," said Ailill to Cormac,
"Go that you may ---- your son.
The cattle do not come from the fields
That the din of the host may not terrify them(?).

'"This will be a battle in its time
For Medb with a third of the host.
There will be flesh of men therefrom
If the Riastartha comes to you."'

Then the Nemain attacked them, and that was not the quietest of nights for them, with the uproar of the churl (i.e. Dubthach) through their sleep. The host started up at once, and a great number of the host were in confusion, till Medb came to reprove him.

Then they went and spent the night in Granard Tethba Tuascirt, after the host had been led astray over bogs and over streams. A warning was sent from Fergus to the Ulstermen here, for friendship. They were now in the weakness, except Cuchulainn and his father Sualtaim.

Cuchulainn and his father went, after the coming of the warning from Fergus, till they were in Iraird Cuillend, watching the host there.

'I think of the host to-night,' said Cuchulainn to his father. 'Go from us with a warning to the Ulstermen. I am forced to go to a tryst with Fedelm Noichride, [Note: Gloss incorporated in the text: that is, with her servant,' etc.] from my own pledge that went out to her.'

He made a spancel-withe [This was a twig twisted in the form of two rings, joined by one straight piece, as used for hobbling horses and cattle.] then before he went, and wrote an ogam on its ----, and threw it on the top of the pillar.

The leadership of the way before the army was given to Fergus. Then Fergus went far astray to the south, till Ulster should have completed the collection of an army; he did this for friendship. Ailill and Medb perceived it; it was then Medb said:

'O Fergus, this is strange,
What kind of way do we go?
Straying south or north
We go over every other folk.

'Ailill of Ai with his hosting
Fears that you will betray them.
You have not given your mind hitherto
To the leading of the way.

'If it is in friendship that you do it,
Do not lead the horses
Peradventure another may be found
To lead the way.'
Fergus replied:

'O Medb, what troubles you?
This is not like treachery.
It belongs to the Ulstermen, O woman,
The land across which I am leading you.

'It is not for the disadvantage of the host
That I go on each wandering in its turn;
It is to avoid the great man
Who protects Mag Murthemne.

'Not that my mind is not distressed
On account of the straying on which I go,
But if perchance I may avoid even afterwards
Cuchulainn Mac Sualtaim.'

Then they went till they were in Iraird Cuillend. Eirr and Indell, Foich and Fo-clam (their two charioteers), the four sons of Iraird Mac Anchinne, [Marginal gloss:

'or the four sons of Nera Mac Nuado Mac Taccain, as it is found in other books.'] it is they who were before the host, to protect their brooches and their cushions and their cloaks, that the dust of the host might not soil them. They found the withe that Cuchulainn threw, and perceived the grazing that the horses had grazed. For Sualtaim's two horses had eaten the grass with its roots from the earth; Cuchulainn's two horses had licked the earth as far as the stones beneath the grass. They sit down then, until the host came, and the musicians play to them. They give the withe into the hands of Fergus Mac Roich; he read the ogam that was on it.

When Medb came, she asked, 'Why are you waiting here?'

'We wait,' said Fergus,' because of the withe yonder. There is an ogam on its ----, and this is what is in it: "Let no one go past till a man is found to throw a like withe with his one hand, and let it be one twig of which it is made; and I except my friend Fergus." Truly,' said Fergus, 'Cuchulainn has thrown it, and they are his horses that grazed the plain.'

And he put it in the hands of the druids; and Fergus sang this song:

'Here is a withe, what does the withe declare to us?
What is its mystery?
What number threw it?
Few or many?

'Will it cause injury to the host,
If they go a journey from it?
Find out, ye druids, something therefore
For what the withe has been left.

'---- of heroes the hero who has thrown it,
Full misfortune on warriors;
A delay of princes, wrathful is the matter,
One man has thrown it with one hand.

'Is not the king's host at the will of him,
Unless it breaks fair play?

Until one man only of you
Throw it, as one man has thrown it.
I do not know anything save that
For which the withe should have been put.
Here is a withe.'

Then Fergus said to them: 'If you outrage this withe,' said he, 'or if you go past it, though he be in the custody of a man, or in a house under a lock, the ---- of the man who wrote the ogam on it will reach him, and will slay a goodly slaughter of you before morning, unless one of you throw a like withe.'

'It does not please us, indeed, that one of us should be slain at once,' said Ailill. 'We will go by the neck of the great wood yonder, south of us, and we will not go over it at all.'

The troops hewed down then the wood before the chariots. This is the name of that place, Slechta. It is there that Partraige is. (According to others, the conversation between Medb and Fedelm the prophetess took place there, as we told before; and then it is after the answer she gave to Medb that the wood was cut down; i.e. 'Look for me,' said Medb, 'how my hosting will be.' 'It is difficult to me,' said the maiden; 'I cannot cast my eye over them in the wood.' 'It is ploughland (?) there shall be,' said Medb; 'we will cut down the wood.' Then this was done, so that Slechta was the name of the place.)

They spent the night then in Cul Sibrille; a great snowstorm fell on them, to the girdles of the men and the wheels of the chariots. The rising was early next morning. And it was not the most peaceful of nights for them, with the snow; and they had not prepared food that night. But it was not early when Cuchulainn came from his tryst; he waited to wash and bathe.

Then he came on the track of the host. 'Would that we had not gone there,' said Cuchulainn, 'nor betrayed the Ulstermen; we have let the host go to them unawares. Make us an estimation of the host,' said Cuchulainn to Loeg, 'that we may know the number of the host.'

Loeg did this, and said to Cuchulainn: 'I am confused,' said he, 'I cannot attain this.'

'It would not be confusion that I see, if only I come,' said

Cuchulainn.

'Get into the chariot then,' said Loeg.

Cuchulainn got into the chariot, and put a reckoning over the host for a long time.

'Even you,' said Loeg, 'you do not find it easy.'

'It is easier indeed to me than to you,' said Cuchulainn; 'for I have three gifts, the gifts of eye, and of mind, and of reckoning. I have put a reckoning [Marginal gloss: 'This is one of the three severest and most difficult reckonings made in Ireland; i.e. Cuchulainn's reckoning of the men of Ireland on the *Tain*; and ug's reckoning of the Fomorian hosts at the battle of Mag Tured; and Ingcel's reckoning of the hosts at the Bruiden Da Derga.'] on this,' said he; 'there are eighteen cantreds,' said he, 'for their number; only that the eighteenth cantred is distributed among all the host, so that their number is not clear; that is, the cantred of the Leinstermen.'

Then Cuchulainn went round the host till he was at Ath Gabla. [Note: LU has Ath Grena.] He cuts a fork [Note: i.e. fork of a tree.] there with one blow of his sword, and put it on the middle of the stream, so that a chariot could not pass it on this side or that. Eirr and Indell, Foich and Fochlam (their two charioteers) came upon him thereat. He strikes their four heads off, and throws them on to the four points of the fork. Hence is Ath Gabla.

Then the horses of the four went to meet the host, and their cushions very red on them. They supposed it was a battalion that was before them at the ford. A troop went from them to look at the ford; they saw nothing there but the track of one chariot and the fork with the four heads, and a name in ogam written on the side. All the host came then.

'Are the heads yonder from our people?' said Medb.

'They are from our people and from our choice warriors,' said Ailill.

One of them read the ogam that was on the side of the fork; that is: 'A man has thrown the fork with his one hand; and you shall not go past it till one of you, except Fergus, has thrown it with one hand.'

'It is a marvel,' said Ailill, 'the quickness with which the four were struck.'

It was not that that was a marvel,' said Fergus; 'it was the striking of the fork from the trunk with one blow; and if the end was [cut] with one blow, [Note: Lit. 'if its end was one cutting.'] it is the fairer for it, and that it was thrust in in this manner; for it is not a hole that has been dug for it, but it is from the back of the chariot it has been thrown with one hand.'

'Avert this strait from us, O Fergus,' said Medb.

Bring me a chariot then,' said Fergus, 'that I may take it out, that you may see whether its end was hewn with one blow.' Fergus broke then fourteen chariots of his chariots, so that it was from his own chariot that he took it out of the ground, and he saw that the end was hewn with one blow.

'Heed must be taken to the character of the tribe to which we are going,' said Ailill. 'Let each of you prepare his food; you had no rest last night for the snow. And something shall be told to us of the adventures and stories of the tribe to which we are going.'

It is then that the adventures of Cuchulainn were related to them. Ailill asked: 'Is it Conchobar who has done this?'

'Not he,' said Fergus; 'he would not have come to the border of the country without the number of a battalion round him.'

'Was it Celtchar Mac Uithidir?'

'Not he; he would not have come to the border of the country without the number of a battalion round him.'

'Was it Eogan Mac Durtacht?'

'Not he,' said Fergus; 'he would not have come over the border of the country without thirty chariots two-pointed (?) round him. This is the man who would have done the deed,' said Fergus, 'Cuchulainn; it is he who would have cut the tree at one blow from the trunk, and who would have killed the four yonder as quickly as they were killed, and who would have come to the boundary with his charioteer.'

'What kind of man,' said Ailill, 'is this Hound of whom we have heard among the Ulstermen? What age is this youth who is famous?'

'An easy question, truly,' said Fergus. 'In his fifth year he went to the boys at Emain Macha to play; in his sixth year he went to learn arms and feats with Scathach. In his seventh year he took arms. He is now seventeen years old at this time.'

'Is it he who is hardest to deal with among the Ulstermen?' said Medb.

'Over every one of them,' said Fergus. 'You will not find before you a warrior who is harder to deal with, nor a point that is sharper or keener or swifter, nor a hero who is fiercer, nor a raven that is more flesh-loving, nor a match of his age that can equal him as far as a third; nor a lion that is fiercer, nor a fence(?) of battle, nor a hammer of destruction, nor a door of battle, nor judgment on hosts, nor preventing of a great host that is more worthy. You will not find there a man who would reach his age, and his growth, and his dress, and his terror, his speech, his splendour, his fame, his voice, his form, his power, his hardness, his accomplishment, his valour, his striking, his rage, his anger, his victory, his doom-giving, his violence, his estimation, his hero-triumph, his speed, his pride, his madness, with the feat of nine men on every point, like Cuchulainn!'

'I don't care for that,' said Medb; 'he is in one body; he endures wounding; he is not above capturing. Therewith his age is that of a grown-up girl, and his manly deeds have not come yet.'

'Not so,' said Fergus. 'It would be no wonder if he were to do a good deed to-day; for even when he was younger his deeds were manly.'

HERE ARE HIS BOYISH DEEDS

'He was brought up,' said Fergus, 'by his mother and father at the ---- in Mag Murthemne. The stories of the boys in Emain were related to him; for there are three fifties of boys there,' said Fergus, 'at play. It is thus that Conchobar enjoys his sovereignty: a third of the day watching the boys; another third playing chess; [Note: *Fidchill*, usually so translated, but the exact nature of the game is uncertain.] another third drinking beer till sleep seizes him therefrom. Although we are in exile, there is not in Ireland a warrior who is more wonderful,' said Fergus.

'Cuchulainn asked his mother then to let him go to the boys.

'"You shall not go," said his mother, "until you have company of warriors."

'"I deem it too long to wait for it," said Cuchulainn. "Show me on which side Emain is."

'"Northwards so," said his mother; "and the journey is hard," said she, "Sliab Fuait is between you."

'"I will find it out," said Cuchulainn.

'He goes forth then, and his shield of lath with him, and his toy-spear, and his playing-club, and his ball. He kept throwing his staff before him, so that he took it by the point before the end fell on the ground.

'He goes then to the boys without binding them to protect him. For no one used to go to them in their play-field till his protection was guaranteed. He did not know this.

'"The boy insults us," said Follomon Mac Conchobair, "besides we know he is of the Ulstermen. ... Throw at him!"

'They throw their three fifties of toy-spears at him, and they all remained standing in his shield of lath. Then they throw all the balls at him; and he takes them, each single ball, in his bosom. Then they throw their three fifties of hurling-clubs at him; he warded them off so that they did not touch him, and he took a bundle of them on his back. Then contortion seized him. You would have thought that it was a hammering wherewith each little hair had been driven into his head, with the arising with which he arose. You would have thought there was a spark of fire on every single hair. He shut one of his eyes so that it was not wider than the eye of a needle. He opened the other so that it was as large as the mouth of a meadcup. He laid bare from his jawbone to his ear; he opened his mouth to his jaw [Note: Conjectured from the later description of Cuchulainn's distortion.] so that his gullet was visible. The hero's light rose from his head. Then he strikes at the boys. He overthrows fifty of them before they reached the door of Emain. Nine of them came over me and Conchobar as we were playing chess. Then he springs over the chessboard after the nine. Conchobar caught his elbow.

'"The boys are not well treated," said Conchobar.

'"Lawful for me, O friend Conchobar," said he. "I came to them from my home to play, from my mother and father; and they have not been good to me."

'"What is your name?" said Conchobar.

'"Setanta Mac Sualtaim am I," said he, "and the son of Dechtere, your sister. It was not fitting to hurt me here."

'"Why were the boys not bound to protect you?" said Conchobar.

'"I did not know this," said Cuchulainn. "Undertake my protection against them then."

'"I recognise it," said Conchobar.

'Then he turned aside on [Note: i.e. to attack them.] the boys throughout the house.

'"What ails you at them now?" said Conchobar.

'"That I may be bound to protect them," said Cuchulainn.

'"Undertake it," said Conchobar.

'"I recognise it," said Cuchulainn.

'Then they all went into the play-field, and those boys who had been struck down there arose. Their foster-mothers and foster-fathers helped them.

'Once,' said Fergus, 'when he was a youth, he used not to sleep in Emain Macha till morning.

'"Tell me," said Conchobar to him, "why you do not sleep?"

'"I do not do it," said Cuchulainn, "unless it is equally high at my head and my feet."

'Then a stone pillar was put by Conchobar at his head, and another at his feet, and a bed was made for him separately between them.

'Another time a certain man went to awaken him, and he struck him with his fist in his forehead, so that it took the front of his forehead on to the brain, and so that he overthrew the pillar with his arm.'

'It is known,' said Ailill, 'that it was the fist of a warrior and that it was the arm of a hero.'

'From that time,' said Fergus, 'no one dared to waken him till he awoke of himself.

'Another time he was playing ball in the play-field east of Emain; he alone apart against the three fifties of boys; he used to defeat them in every game in this way always. The boys lay hold of him therewith, and he plied his fist upon them until fifty of them were killed. He took to flight then, till he was under the pillow of Conchobar's bed. All the Ulstermen rise round him, and I rise, and Conchobar himself. Then he rose under the bed, and put the bed from him, with the thirty heroes who were on it, till it was in the middle of the house. The Ulstermen sit round him in the house. We arrange and make peace then,' said Fergus, 'between the boys and him.

'There was contention between Ulster and Eogan Mac Durtacht. The Ulstermen went to the battle. He was left asleep. The Ulstermen were defeated. Conchobar was left [on the field], and Cuscraid Mend Macha, and many more beside. Their lament awoke Cuchulainn. He stretched himself then, so that the two stones that were about him broke; in the presence of Bricriu yonder it was done,' said Fergus. 'Then he arose. I met him in the door of the fort, and I wounded.

'"Alas! God save you, friend Fergus," said he, "where is Conchobar?"

'"I do not know," said I.

'Then he went forth. The night was dark. He made for the battlefield. He saw a man before him, with half his head on, and half of another man on his back.

'"Help me, O Cuchulainn," said he; "I have been wounded and I have brought half of my brother on my back. Carry it for me a while."

'"I will not carry it," said he.

'Then he throws the burden to him; he throws it from him; they wrestle; Cuchulainn was overthrown. I heard something, the Badb from the corpses: "Ill the stuff of a hero that is under the feet of a phantom." Then Cuchulainn rose against him, and strikes his head off with his playing-club, and begins to drive his ball before him across the plain.

'"Is my friend Conchobar in this battlefield?"

'He answered him. He goes to him, till he sees him in the trench, and there was the earth round him on every side to hide him.

'"Why have you come into the battlefield," said Conchobar, "that you may swoon there?"

'He lifts him out of the trench then; six of the strong men of Ulster with us would not have brought him out more bravely.

'"Go before us to the house yonder," said Conchobar; "if a roast pig came to me, I should live."

'"I will go and bring it," said Cuchulainn.

'He goes then, and saw a man at a cooking-hearth in the middle of the wood; one of his two hands had his weapons in it, the other was cooking the pig.

'The hideousness of the man was great; nevertheless he attacked him and took his head and his pig with him. Conchobar ate the pig then.

'"Let us go to our house," said Conchobar.

'They met Cuscraid Mac Conchobair. There were sure wounds on him; Cuchulainn took him on his back. The three of them went then to Emain Macha.

'Another time the Ulstermen were in their weakness. There was not among us,' said Fergus, 'weakness on women and boys, nor on any one who was outside the country of the Ulstermen, nor on Cuchulainn and his father. And so no one dared to shed their blood; for the suffering springs on him who wounds them. [Gloss incorporated in text: 'or their decay, or their shortness of life.']

'Three times nine men came to us from the Isles of Faiche. They went over our back court when we were in our weakness. The women screamed in the court. The boys were in the play-field; they come at the cries. When the boys saw the dark, black men, they all take to flight except Cuchulainn alone. He plies hand-stones and his playing-club on them. He kills nine of them, and they leave fifty wounds on him, and they go forth besides. A man who did these deeds when his five years were not full, it would be no wonder that he should have come to the edge of the boundary and that he should have cut off the heads of yonder four.'

'We know him indeed, this boy,' said Conall Cernach, 'and we know him none the worse that he is a fosterling of ours. It was not long after the deed that Fergus has just related, when he did another deed. When Culann the smith served a feast to Conchobar, Culann said that it was not a multitude that should be brought to him, for the preparation which he had made was not from land or country, but from the fruit of his two hands and his pincers. Then Conchobar went, and fifty chariots with him, of those who were noblest and most eminent of the heroes. Now Conchobar visited then his play-field. It was always his custom to visit and revisit them at going and coming, to seek a greeting of the boys. He saw then Cuchulainn driving his ball against the three fifties of boys, and he gets the victory over them. When it was hole-driving that they did, he filled the hole with his balls and they could not ward him off. When they were all throwing into the hole, he warded them off alone, so that not a single ball would go in it. When it was wrestling they were doing, he overthrew the three fifties of boys by himself, and there did not meet round him a number that could overthrow him. When it was stripping that they did, he stripped them all so that they were quite naked, and they could not take from him even his brooch out of his cloak.

'Conchobar thought this wonderful. He said "Would he bring his deeds to completion, provided the age of manhood came to them?" Every one said: "He would bring them to completion." Conchobar said to Cuchulainn: "Come with me," said he, "to the feast to which we are going, because you are a guest."

'"I have not had enough of play yet, O friend Conchobar," said the boy; "I will come after you."

'When they had all come to the feast, Culann said to Conchobar: "Do you expect any one to follow you?" said he.

"'No," said Conchobar. He did not remember the appointment with his foster-son who was following him.

"'I'll have a watch-dog," said Culann; "there are three chains on him, and three men to each chain. [Gloss incorporated in text: 'He was brought from Spain.'] Let him be let slip because of our cattle and stock, and let the court be shut."

'Then the boy comes. The dog attacks him. He went on with his play still: he threw his ball, and threw his club after it, so that it struck the ball. One stroke was not greater than another; and he threw his toy-spear after them, and he caught it before falling; and it did not hinder his play, though the dog was approaching him. Conchobar and his retinue ---- this, so that they could not move; they thought they would not find him alive when they came, even though the court were open. Now when the dog came to him, he threw away his ball and his club, and seized the dog with his two hands; that is, he put one of his hands to the apple of the dog's throat; and he put the other at its back; he struck it against the pillar that was beside him, so that every limb sprang apart. (According to another, it was his ball that he threw into its mouth, and brought out its entrails through it.)

'The Ulstermen went towards him, some over the wall, others over the doors of the court. They put him on Conchobar's knee. A great clamour arose among them, that the king's sister's son should have been almost killed. Then Culann comes into the house.

"'Welcome, boy, for the sake of your mother. Would that I had not prepared a feast! My life is a life lost, and my husbandry is a husbandry without, without my dog. He had kept honour and life for me," said he, "the man of my household who has been taken from me, that is, my dog. He was defence and protection to our property and our cattle; he was the protection of every beast to us, both field and house."

"'It is not a great matter," said the boy; "a whelp of the same litter shall be raised for you by me, and I will be a dog for the defence of your cattle and for your own defence now, until that dog grows, and until he is capable of action; and I will defend Mag Murthemne, so that there shall not be taken away from me cattle nor herd, unless I have ----."

"'Then your name shall be Cu-chulainn," said Cathbad.

'"I am content that it may be my name," said Cuchulainn.

'A man who did this in his seventh year, it would be no wonder that he should have done a great deed now when his seventeen years are completed,' said Conall Cernach.

'He did another exploit,' said Fiacha Mac Fir-Febe. 'Cathbad the Druid was with his son, Conchobar Mac Nessa. A hundred active men were with him, learning magic from him. That is the number that Cathbad used to teach. A certain one of his pupils asked of him for what this day would be good. Cathbad said a warrior should take arms therein whose name should be over Ireland for ever, for deed of valour, and his fame should continue for ever. Cuchulainn heard this. He comes to Conchobar to ask for arms. Conchobar said, "Who has instructed you?"

'"My friend Cathbad," said Cuchulainn.

'"We know indeed," said Conchobar.

'He gave him spear and shield. He brandished them in the middle of the house, so that nothing remained of the fifteen sets of armour that were in store in Conchobar's household against the breaking of weapons or taking of arms by any one. Conchobar's own armour was given to him. That withstood him, and he brandished it, and blessed the king whose armour it was, and said, "Blessing to the people and race to whom is king the man whose armour that is."

'Then Cathbad came to them, and said: "Has the boy taken arms?" said Cathbad.

'"Yes," said Conchobar.

'"This is not lucky for the son of his mother," said he.

'"What, is it not you advised it?" said Conchobar.

'"Not I, surely," said Cathbad.

'"What advantage to you to deceive me, wild boy?" said Conchobar to Cuchulainn.

'"O king of heroes, it is no trick," said Cuchulainn; "it is he who taught it to his pupils this morning; and I heard him, south of Emain, and I came to you then."

'"The day is good thus," said Cathbad; "it is certain he will be famous and renowned, who shall take arms therein; but he will be short-lived only."

'"A wonder of might," said Cuchulainn; "provided I be famous, I am content though I were but one day in the world."

'Another day a certain man asked the druids what it is for which that day was good.

'"Whoever shall go into a chariot therein," said Cathbad, "his name shall be over Ireland for ever."

'Then Cuchulainn heard this; he comes to Conchobar and said to him: "O friend Conchobar," said he, "give me a chariot." He gave him a chariot. He put his hand between the two poles [Note: The *fertais* were poles sticking out behind the chariot, as the account of the wild deer, later, shows.] of the chariot, so that the chariot broke. He broke twelve chariots in this way. Then Conchobar's chariot was given to him. This withstood him. He goes then in the chariot, and Conchobar's charioteer with him. The charioteer (Ibor was his name) turned the chariot under him. "Come out of the chariot now," said the charioteer.

'"The horses are fine, and I am fine, their little lad," said Cuchulainn. "Go forward round Emain only, and you shall have a reward for it."

'So the charioteer goes, and Cuchulainn forced him then that he should go on the road to greet the boys "and that the boys might bless me."

'He begged him to go on the way again. When they come, Cuchulainn said to the charioteer: "Ply the goad on the horses," said he.

'"In what direction?" said the charioteer.

'"As long as the road shall lead us," said Cuchulainn.

'They come thence to Sliab Fuait, and find Conall Cernach there. It fell to Conall that day to guard the province; for every hero of Ulster was in Sliab Fuait in turn, to protect any one who should come with poetry, or to fight against a man; so that it should be there that there should be some one to encounter him, that no one should go to Emain unperceived.

'"May that be for prosperity," said Conall; "may it be for victory and triumph."

'"Go to the fort, O Conall, and leave me to watch here now," said Cuchulainn.

'"It will be enough," said Conall, "if it is to protect any one with poetry; if it is to fight against a man, it is early for you yet."

'"Perhaps it may not be necessary at all," said Cuchulainn. "Let us go meanwhile," said Cuchulainn, "to look upon the edge of Loch Echtra. Heroes are wont to abide there."

'"I am content," said Conall.

'Then they go thence. He throws a stone from his sling, so that a pole of Conall

Cernach's chariot breaks.

'"Why have you thrown the stone, O boy?" said Conall.

"To try my hand and the straightness of my throw," said Cuchulainn; "and it is the custom with you Ulstermen, that you do not travel beyond your peril. Go back to Emain, O friend Conall, and leave me here to watch."

'"Content, then," said Conall.

'Conall Cernach did not go past the place after that. Then Cuchulainn goes forth to Loch Echtra, and they found no one there before them. The charioteer said to Cuchulainn that they should go to Emain, that they might be in time for the drinking there.

'"No," said Cuchulainn. "What mountain is it yonder?" said Cuchulainn.

'"Sliab Monduirn," said the charioteer.

'"Let us go and get there," said Cuchulainn. They go then till they reach it. When they had reached the mountain, Cuchulainn asked: "What is the white cairn yonder on the top of the mountain?"

'"Find Carn," said the charioteer.

'"What plain is that over there?" said Cuchulainn.

'"Mag Breg," said the charioteer. He tells him then the name of every chief fort between Temair and Cenandas. He tells him first their meadows and their fords, their famous places and their dwellings, their fortresses and their high hills. He shows [Note: Reading with YBL.] him then the fort of the three sons of Nechta Scene; Foill, Fandall, and Tuachell were their names.

'"Is it they who say," said Cuchulainn, "that there are not more of the Ulstermen alive than they have slain of them?"

'"It is they indeed," said the charioteer.

'"Let us go till we reach them," said Cuchulainn.

'"Indeed it is peril to us," said the charioteer.

'"Truly it is not to avoid it that we go," said Cuchulainn.

'Then they go forth and unharness their horses at the meeting of the bog and the river, to the south above the fort of the others; and he threw the withe that was on the pillar as far as he could throw into the river and let it go with the stream, for this was a breach of *geis* to the sons of Nechta Scene. They perceive it then, and come to them. Cuchulainn goes to sleep by the pillar after throwing the withe at the stream; and he said to the charioteer: "Do not waken me for few; but waken me for many."

'Now the charioteer was very frightened, and he made ready their chariot and pulled its coverings and skins which were over Cuchulainn; for he dared not waken him, because Cuchulainn told him at first that he should not waken him for a few.

'Then come the sons of Nechta Scene.

'"Who is it who is there?" said one of them.

'"A little boy who has come to-day into the chariot for an expedition," said the charioteer.

'"May it not be for his happiness," said the champion; "and may it not be for his prosperity, his first taking of arms. Let him not be in our land, and let the horses not graze there any more," said the champion.

'"Their reins are in my hands," said the charioteer.

'"It should not be yours to earn hatred," said Ibar to the champion; "and the boy is asleep."

'"I am not a boy at all," said Cuchulainn; "but it is to seek battle with a man that the boy who is here has come."

'"That pleases me well," said the champion.

'"It will please you now in the ford yonder," said Cuchulainn.

'"It befits you," said the charioteer, "take heed of the man who comes against you. Foill is his name," said he; "for unless you reach him in the first thrust, you will not reach him till evening."

'"I swear by the god by whom my people swear, he will not ply his skill on the Ulstermen again, if the broad spear of my friend Conchobar should reach him from my hand. It will be an outlaw's hand to him."

'Then he cast the spear at him, so that his back broke. He took with him his accoutrements and his head.

'"Take heed of another man," said the charioteer, "Fandall [Note: i.e. 'Swallow.'] is his name. Not more heavily does he traverse(?) the water than swan or swallow."

'"I swear that he will not ply that feat again on the Ulstermen," said Cuchulainn. "You have seen," said he, "the way I travel the pool at Emain."

'They meet then in the ford. Cuchulainn kills that man, and took his head and his arms.

'"Take heed of another man who comes towards you," said the charioteer. "Tuachell [Note: i.e. 'Cunning.'] is his name. It is no misname for him, for he does not fall by arms at all."

'"Here is the javelin for him to confuse him, so that it may make a red-sieve of him," said Cuchulainn.

'He cast the spear at him, so that it reached him in his ----. Then He went to him and cut off his head. Cuchulainn gave his head and his accoutrements to his own charioteer. He heard then the cry of their mother, Nechta Scene, behind them.

'He puts their spoils and the three heads in his chariot with him, and said: "I will not leave my triumph," said he, "till I reach Emain Macha." 'then they set out with his triumph.

'Then Cuchulainn said to the charioteer: "You promised us a good run," said he, "and we need it now because of the strife and the pursuit that is behind us." They go on to Sliab Fuait; and such was the speed of the run that they made over Breg after the spurring of the charioteer, that the horses of the chariot overtook the wind and the birds in flight, and that Cuchulainn caught the throw that he sent from his sling before it reached the ground.

'When they reached Sliab Fuait, they found a herd of wild deer there before them.

'"What are those cattle yonder so active?" said Cuchulainn.

'"Wild deer," said the charioteer.

'"Which would the Ulstermen think best," said Cuchulainn, "to bring them dead or alive?"

'"It is more wonderful alive," said the charioteer; "it is not every one who can do it so. Dead, there is not one of them who cannot do it. You cannot do this, to carry off any of them alive," said the charioteer.

'"I can indeed," said Cuchulainn. "Ply the goad on the horses into the bog."

'The charioteer does this. The horses stick in the bog. Cuchulainn sprang down and seized the deer that was nearest, and that was the finest of them. He lashed the horses through the bog, and overcame the deer at once, and bound it between the two poles of the chariot.

'They saw something again before them, a flock of swans.

"'Which would the Ulstermen think best," said Cuchulainn, "to have them dead or alive?"

"'All the most vigorous and finest(?) bring them alive," said the charioteer.

'Then Cuchulainn aims a small stone at the birds, so that he struck eight of the birds. He threw again a large stone, so that he struck twelve of them. All that was done by his return stroke.

"Collect the birds for us," said Cuchulainn to his charioteer. "If it is I who go to take them," said he, "the wild deer will spring upon you."

"'It is not easy for me to go to them," said the charioteer. "The horses have become wild so that I cannot go past them. I cannot go past the two iron tyres [Interlinear gloss, *fonnod*. The *fonnod* was some part of the rim of the wheel apparently.] of the chariot, because of their sharpness; and I cannot go past the deer, for his horn has filled all the space between the two poles of the chariot."

"'Step from its horn," said Cuchulainn. "I swear by the god by whom the Ulstermen swear, the bending with which I will bend my head on him, and the eye that I will make at him, he will not turn his head on you, and he will not dare to move."

'That was done then. Cuchulainn made fast the reins, and the charioteer collects the birds. Then Cuchulainn bound the birds from the strings and thongs of the chariot; so that it was thus he went to Emain Macha: the wild deer behind his chariot, and the flock of swans flying over it, and the three heads in his chariot. Then they come to Emain.

"A man in a chariot is coming to you," said the watchman in Emain Macha; "he will shed the blood of every man who is in the court, unless heed is taken, and unless naked women go to him."

'Then he turned the left side of his chariot towards Emain, and that was a *geis* [Note: i.e. it was an insult.] to it; and Cuchulainn said: "I swear by the god by whom the Ulstermen swear, unless a man is found to fight with me, I will shed the blood of every one who is in the fort."

"'Naked women to meet him!" said Conchobar.

'Then the women of Emain go to meet him with Mugain, the wife of Conchobar Mac Nessa, and bare their breasts before him. "These are the warriors who will meet you to-day," said Mugain.

'He covers his face; then the heroes of Emain seize him and throw him into a vessel of cold water. That vessel bursts round him. The second vessel into which he was thrown boiled with bubbles as big as the fist therefrom. The third vessel into which he went, he warmed it so that its heat and its cold were rightly tempered. Then he comes out; and the queen, Mugain, puts a blue mantle on him, and a silver brooch therein, and a hooded tunic; and he sits at Conchobar's knee, and that was his couch always after that. The man who did this in his seventh year,' said Fiacha Mac Fir-Febe, 'it were not wonderful though he should rout an overwhelming force, and though he should exhaust (?) an equal force, when his seventeen years are complete to-day.'

(What follows is a separate version [Note: The next episode, the Death of Fraech, is not given in LL.] to the death of Orlam.)

'Let us go forth now,' said Ailill.

Then they reached Mag Mucceda. Cuchulainn cut an oak before them there, and wrote an ogam in its side. It is this that was therein: that no one should go past it till a warrior should leap it with one chariot. They pitch their tents there, and come to leap over it in their chariots. There fall thereat thirty horses, and thirty chariots are broken. Belach n-Ane, that is the name of that place for ever.

The Death of Fraech

They are there till next morning; then Fraech is summoned to them. 'Help us, O Fraech,' said Medb. 'Remove from us the strait that is on us. Go before Cuchulainn for us, if perchance you shall fight with him.'

He set out early in the morning with nine men, till he reached Ath Fuait. He saw the warrior bathing in the river.

'Wait here,' said Fraech to his retinue, ''till I come to the man yonder; not good is the water,' said he.

He took off his clothes, and goes into the water to him.

'Do not come to me,' said Cuchulainn. 'You will die from it, and I should be sorry to kill you.'

'I shall come indeed,' said Fraech, 'that we may meet in the water; and let your play with me be fair.'

'Settle it as you like,' said Cuchulainn.

'The hand of each of us round the other,' said Fraech.

They set to wrestling for a long time on the water, and Fraech was submerged. Cuchulainn lifted him up again.

'This time,' said Cuchulainn, 'will you yield and accept your life?' [Note: Lit. 'will you acknowledge your saving?']

'I will not suffer it,' said Fraech.

Cuchulainn put him under it again, until Fraech was killed. He comes to land; his retinue carry his body to the camp. Ath Fraich, that was the name of that ford for ever. All the host lamented Fraech. They saw a troop of women in green tunics [Note: Fraech was descended from the people of the Sid, his mother Bebind being a fairy woman. Her sister was Boinn (the river Boyne).] on the body of Fraech Mac Idaid; they drew him from them into the mound. Sid Fraich was the name of that mound afterwards.

Fergus springs over the oak in his chariot. They go till they reach Ath Taiten; Cuchulainn destroys six of them there: that is, the six Dungals of Irress.

Then they go on to Fornocht. Medb had a whelp named Baiscne. Cuchulainn throws a cast at him, and took his head off. Druim was the name of that place henceforth.

'Great is the mockery to you,' said Medb, 'not to hunt the deer of misfortune yonder that is killing you.'

Then they start hunting him, till they broke the shafts of their chariots thereat.

The Death of Orlam

They go forth then over Iraird Culend in the morning. Cuchulainn went forward; he overtook the charioteer of Orlam, son of Ailill and Medb, in Tamlacht Orlaim, a little to the north of Disert Lochait, cutting wood there. (According to another version, it is The shaft of Cuchulainn's chariot that had broken, and it is to cut a shaft that he had gone when he met Orlam's charioteer. It is the charioteer who cut the shafts according to this version.)

'It is over-bold what the Ulstermen are doing, if it is they who are yonder,' said Cuchulainn, 'while the host is behind them.' He goes to the charioteer to reprove him; he thought that he was of Ulster, and he saw the man cutting wood, that is the chariot shaft.

'What are you doing here?' said Cuchulainn.

'Cutting chariot-shafts,' said the charioteer. 'We have broken our chariots hunting the wild deer Cuchulainn yonder. Help me,' said the charioteer. 'Look only whether you are to select the shafts, or to strip them.'

'It will be to strip them indeed,' said Cuchulainn.

Then Cuchulainn stripped the shafts through his fingers in the presence of the other, so that he cleared them both of bark and knots.

'This cannot be your proper work that I put on you,' said the charioteer; he was greatly afraid.

'Whence are you?' said Cuchulainn.

'The charioteer of Orlam, son of Ailill and Medb,' said he. 'And you?' said the charioteer.

'My name is Cuchulainn,' said he.

'Alas!' said the charioteer.

'Fear nothing,' said Cuchulainn. 'Where is your master?' said he.

'He is in the trench yonder,' said the charioteer.

'Go forth then with me,' said Cuchulainn, 'for I do not kill charioteers at all.'

Cuchulainn goes to Orlam, kills him, cuts his head off, and shakes his head before the host. Then he puts the head on the charioteer's back, and said to him:

'Take that with you,' said Cuchulainn, 'and go to the camp thus. If you do not go thus, a stone will come to you from my sling.'

When he got near the camp, he took the head from his back, and told his adventures to Ailill and Medb.

'This is not like taking birds,' said she.

And he said, 'Unless I brought it on my back to the camp, he would break my head with a stone.'

The Death of the Meic Garach

Then the Meic Garach waited on their ford. These are their names: Lon and Ualu and Diliu; and Mes-Ler, and Mes-Laech, and Mes-Lethan were their three charioteers. They thought it too much what Cuchulainn had done: to slay two foster-sons of the king, and his son, and to shake the head before the host. They would slay Cuchulainn in return for him, and would themselves remove this annoyance from the host. They cut three aspen wands for their charioteers, that the six of them should pursue combat against him. He killed them all then, because they had broken fair-play towards him.

Orlam's charioteer was then between Ailill and Medb. Cuchulainn hurled a stone at him, [Note: Apparently because the charioteer had not carried Orlam's head into the camp on his back. Or an alternative version.] so that his head broke, and his brains came over his ears; Fertedil was his name. (Thus it is not true that Cuchulainn did not kill charioteers; howbeit, he did not kill them without fault.)

The Death of the Squirrel

Cuchulainn threatened in Methe, that wherever he should see Ailill or Medb afterwards he would throw a stone from his sling at them. He did this then: he threw a stone from his sling, so that he killed the squirrel that was on Medb's shoulder south of the ford: hence is Methe Togmaill. And he killed the bird that was on Ailill's shoulder north of the ford: hence is Methe n-Eoin. (Or it is on Medb's shoulder that both squirrel and bird were together, and it is their heads that were struck from them by the casts.)

Reoin was drowned in his lake. Hence is Loch Reoin.

'That other is not far from you,' said Ailill to the Manes.

They arose and looked round. When they sat down again, Cuchulainn struck one of them, so that his head broke.

'It was well that you went for that: your boasting was not fitting,' said Maenen the fool. 'I would have taken his head off.'

Cuchulainn threw a stone at him, so that his head broke. It is thus then that these were killed: Orlam in the first place on his hill; the Meic Garach on their ford; Fertedil in his ---; Maenan in his hill.

'I swear by the god by whom my people swear,' said Ailill, 'that man who shall make a mock of Cuchulainn here, I will make two halves of him.'

'Go forth for us both day and night,' said Ailill, 'till we reach Cualnge. That man will kill two-thirds of the host in this way.' It is there that the harpers of the *Cainbili* [Note: Reference obscure. They were wizards of some sort.] from Ossory came to them to amuse them. They thought it was from the Ulstermen to spy on them. They set to hunting them, till they went before them in the forms of deer into the stones at Liac Mor on the north. For they were wizards with great cunning.

The Death of Lethan

Lethan came on to his ford on the Nith (?) in Conaille. He waited himself to meet Cuchulainn. It vexed him what Cuchulainn had done. Cuchulainn cuts off his head and left it, hence it is Ath Lethan on the Nith. And their chariots broke in the battle on the ford by him; hence it is Ath Carpat. Mulcha, Lethan's charioteer, fell on the shoulder of the hill that is between them; hence is Gulo Mulchai. While the hosts were going over Mag Breg, he struck(?) their ---- still. [Note: 2 Something apparently missing here. The passage in LL is as follows: 'It is the same day that the Morrigan, daughter of Ernmas, came from the Sid, so that she was on the pillar in Temair Cuailnge, taking a warning to the Dun of Cualnge before the men of Ireland, and she began to speak to him, and "Good, O wretched one, O Dun of Cualnge," said the Morrigan, "keep watch, for the men of Ireland have reached thee, and they will take thee to their camp unless thou keepest watch"; and she began to take a warning to him thus, and uttered her words on high.' (The Rhetoric follows as in LU.)]

Yet that was the Morrigan in the form of a bird on the pillar in Temair Cuailnge; and she spoke to the Bull:

'Does the Black know,' etc. [Note: A Rhetoric.]

Then the Bull went, and fifty heifers with him, to Sliab Culind; and his keeper, Forgemen by name, went after him. He threw off the three fifties of boys who used always to play on him, and he killed two-thirds of his boys, and dug a trench in Tir Marcceni in Cualnge before he went.

The Death of Lochu

Cuchulainn killed no one from the Saile ind Orthi (?) in the Conaille territory, until they reached Cualnge. Cuchulainn was then in Cuince; he threatened then that when he saw Medb he would throw a stone at her head. This was not easy to him, for it is thus that Medb went and half the host about her, with their shelter of shields over her head.

Then a waiting-woman of Medb's, Lochu by name, went to get water, and a great troop of women with her. Cuchulainn thought it was Medb. He threw two stones from Cuince, so that he slew her in her plain(?). Hence is Ath Rede Locha in Cualnge.

From Findabair Cuailnge the hosts divided, and they set the country on fire. They collect all there were of women, and boys, and maidens; and cattle, in Cualnge together, so that they were all in Findabair.

'You have not gone well,' said Medb; 'I do not see the Bull with you.'

'He is not in the province at all,' said every one.

Lothar the cowherd is summoned to Medb.

'Where is the Bull?' said she. 'Have you an idea?'

'I have great fear to tell it,' said the herd. 'The night,' said he, 'when the Ulster-men went into their weakness, he went with three twenties of heifers with him, so that he is at the Black Corrie of Glenn Gatt.'

'Go,' said Medb, 'and carry a withe [Note: Ir. **gatt**, a withe.] between each two of you.'

They do this: hence this glen is called Glenn Gatt. Then they bring the Bull to Findabair. The place where he saw the herd, Lothar, he attacked him, so that he brought his entrails out on his horns; and he attacked the camp with his three fifties of heifers, so that fifty warriors were killed. And that is the death of Lothar on the Foray.

Then the Bull went from them out of the camp, and they knew not where he had gone from them; and they were ashamed. Medb asked the herd if he had an idea where the Bull was.

'I think he would be in the secret places of Sliab Culind.'

When they returned thus after ravaging Cualnge, and did not find the Bull there. The river Cronn rose against them to the tops of the trees; and they spent the night by it. And Medb told part of her following to go across.

A wonderful warrior went next day, Ualu his name. He took a great stone on his back to go across the water; the stream drove him backwards with the stone on his back. His grave and his stone are on the road at the stream: Lia Ualand is its name.

They went round the river Cronn to the source, and they would have gone between the source and the mountain, only that they could not get leave from Medb; she preferred to go across the mountain, that their track might remain there for ever, for an insult to the Ulstermen. They waited there three days and three nights, till they dug the earth in front of them, the Bernas Bo Cuailnge.

It is there that Cuchulainn killed Crond and Coemdele and ---- [Note: Obscure.]. A hundred warriors ---- [Note: Obscure.] died with Roan and Roae, the two historians of the Foray. A hundred and forty-four, kings died by him at the same stream. They came then over the Bernas Bo Cuailnge with the cattle and stock of Cualnge, and spent the night in Glenn Dail Imda in Cualnge. Botha is the name of this place, because they made huts over them there. They come next day to Colptha. They try to cross it through heedlessness. It rose against them then, and it carries a hundred charioteers of them to the sea; this is the name of the land in which they were drowned, Cluain Carptech.

They go round Colptha then to its source, to Belat Alioin, and spent the night at Liasa Liac; that is the name of this place, because they made sheds over their calves there between Cualnge and Conaille. They came over Glenn Gatlaig, and Glass Gatlaig rose against them. Sechaire was its name before; Glass Gatlaig thenceforth, because it was in withes they brought their calves; and they slept at Druim Fene in Conaille. (Those then are the wanderings from Cualnge to Machaire according to this version.)

This is the Harrying of Cualnge

(Other authors and books make it that another way was taken on their journeyings from Findabair to Conaille, as follows:

Medb said after every one had come with their booty, so that they were all in Findabair Cuailnge: 'Let the host be divided,' said Medb; 'it will be impossible to bring this expedition by one way. Let Ailill go with half the expedition by Midluachair; Fergus and I will go by Bernas Ulad.' [Note: YBL. Bernas Bo n-Ulad.]

'It is not fine,' said Fergus, 'the half of the expedition that has fallen to us. It will be impossible to bring the cattle over the mountain without dividing it.'

That was done then, so that it is from that there is Bernas Bo n-Ulad.)

It is there then that Ailill said to his charioteer Cuillius: 'Find out for me today Medb and Fergus. I know not what has brought them to this union. I shall be pleased that a token should come to me by you.'

Cuillius came when they were in Cluichre. The pair remained behind, and the warriors went on. Cuillius came to them, and they heard not the spy. Fergus' sword happened to be beside him. Cuillius drew it out of its sheath, and left the sheath empty. Cuillius came to Ailill.

'So?' said Ailill.

'So indeed,' said Cuillius; 'there is a token for you.'

'It is well,' said Ailill.

Each of them smiles at the other.

'As you thought,' said Cuillius, 'it is thus that I found them, in one another's arms.'

'It is right for her,' said Ailill; 'it is for help on the Foray that she has done it. See that the sword is kept in good condition,' said Ailill. 'Put it under your seat in the chariot, and a cloth of linen around it.'

Fergus got up for his sword after that.

'Alas!' said he.

'What is the matter with you?' said Medb.

'An ill deed have I done to Ailill,' said he. 'Wait here, while I go into the wood,' said Fergus; 'and do not wonder though it be long till I come.'

It happened that Medb knew not the loss of the sword. He goes thence, and takes the sword of his charioteer with him in his hand. He makes a wooden sword in the wood. Hence there is Fid Mor Drualle in Ulster.

'Let us go on after our comrades,' said Fergus. All their hosts meet in the plain. They pitch their tents. Fergus is summoned to Ailill to play chess. When Fergus went to the tent, Ailill began to laugh at him. [Note: Here follows about two columns of rhetoric, consisting of a taunting dialogue between Ailill, Fergus and Medb.]

***

Cuchulainn came so that he was at Ath Cruinn before them.

'O friend Loeg,' said he to his charioteer, 'the hosts are at hand to us.'

'I swear by the gods,' said the charioteer, 'I will do a mighty feat before warriors ... on slender steeds with yokes of silver, with golden wheels ...'

'Take heed, O Loeg,' said Cuchulainn; 'hold the reins for great victory of Macha ... I beseech,' said Cuchulainn, 'the waters to help me. I beseech heaven and earth, and the Cronn in particular.'

The (river) Cronn takes to fighting against them; it will not let them into Murthemne until the work of heroes be finished in Sliab Tuath Ochaine.

Therewith the water rose up till it was in the tops of the trees.

Mane, son of Ailill and Medb, went before the rest. Cuchulainn smites them on the ford, and thirty horsemen of Mane's retinue were drowned in the water. Cuchulainn overthrew two sixteens of warriors of them again by the water.

They pitch their tents at that ford. Lugaid Mac Nois, descendant of Lomarc Allchomach, came to speak to Cuchulainn, with thirty horsemen.

'Welcome, O Lugaid,' said Cuchulainn. 'If a flock of birds graze upon Mag Murthemne, you shall have a duck with half of another; if fish come to the estuaries, you shall have a salmon with half of another. You shall have the three sprigs, the sprig of watercress, and the sprig of marshwort, and the sprig of seaweed. You shall have a man in the ford in your place.' [Note: This and the following speech are apparently forms of greeting. Cuchulainn offers Lugaid such hospitality as lies in his power. See a similar speech later to Fergus.]

'I believe it,' said Lugaid. 'Excellence of people to the boy whom I desire.'

'Your hosts are fine,' said Cuchulainn.

It would not be sad for you alone before them,' said Lugaid.

'Fair-play and valour will support me,' said Cuchulainn. 'O friend Lugaid, do the hosts fear me?'

'I swear by God,' said Lugaid, 'one man nor two dare not go out of the camp, unless it be in twenties or thirties.'

'It will be something extra for them,' said Cuchulainn, 'if I take to throwing from the sling. Fitting for you will be this fellow-vassal, O Lugaid, that you have among the Ulstermen, if there come to me the force of every man. Say what you would have,' said Cuchulainn.

'That I may have a truce with you towards my host.'

'You shall have it, provided there be a token on it. And tell my friend Fergus that there be a token on his host. Tell the physicians, let there be a token on their host. And let them swear preservation of life to me, and let there come to me provision every night from them.'

Then Lugaid goes from him. Fergus happened to be in the tent with Ailill. Lugaid called him out, and told him this. Something was heard, namely Ailill. ... [Note: Rhetoric, six lines, the substance of which is, apparently, that Ailill asks protection also.]

'I swear by God I cannot do it,' said Lugaid, 'unless I ask the boy Again.'

'Help me, [Note: Spoken by Fergus?] O Lugaid, go to him to see whether Ailill may come with a cantred into my troop. Take an ox with bacon to him and a jar of wine.'

He goes to Cuchulainn then and tells him this.

'I do not mind though he go,' said Cuchulainn.

Then their two troops join. They are there till night. Cuchulainn kills thirty men of them with the sling. (Or they would be twenty nights there, as some books say.)

'Your journeyings are bad,' said Fergus. 'The Ulstermen will come to you out of their weakness, and they will grind you to earth and gravel. "The corner of battle" in which we are is bad.'

He goes thence to Cul Airthir. It happened that Cuchulainn had gone that night to speak to the Ulstermen [Note: In LL and Y BL this incident occurs later, and the messenger is Sualtaim, not Cuchulainn. LU is clearly wrong here.]

'Have you news?' said Conchobar.

'Women are captured,' said Cuchulainn, 'cattle are driven away, men are slain.'

'Who carries them off? who drives them away? who kills them?'

'... Ailill Mac Matae carries them off, and Fergus Mac Roich very bold ...' [Note: Rhetoric.]

'It is not great profit to you,' said Conchobar, 'to-day, our smiting has come to us all the same.'

Cuchulainn goes thence from them; he saw the hosts going forth.

'Alas,' said Ailill, 'I see chariots' ..., etc [Note: Rhetoric, five lines.]

Cuchulainn kills thirty men of them on Ath Duirn. They could not reach Cul Airthir then till night. He slays thirty of them there, and they pitch their tents there. Ailill's charioteer, Cuillius, was washing the chariot tyres [Note: See previous note on the word *fonnod*; the word used here is *fonnod*.] in the ford in the morning; Cuchulainn struck him with a stone and killed him. Hence is Ath Cuillne in Cul Airthir. They reach Druim Feine in Conaille and spent the night there, as we have said before.

Cuchulainn attacked them there; he slays a hundred men of them every night of the three nights that they were there; he took a sling to them from Ochaine near them.

'Our host will be short-lived through Cuchulainn in this way,' said Ailill. 'Let an agreement be carried from us to him: that he shall have the equal of Mag Murthemne from Mag Ai, and the best chariot that is in Ai, and the equipment of twelve men. Offer, if it pleases him better, the plain in which he was brought up, and three sevens of cumals [Note: The *cumal* (bondmaid) was a standard of value.]; and everything that has been destroyed of his household (?) and cattle shall be made good, and he shall have full compensation (?), and let him go into my service; it is better for him than the service of a sub king.'

'Who shall go for that?'

'Mac Roth yonder.'

Mac Roth, the messenger of Ailill and Medb, went on that errand to Delga: it is he who encircles Ireland in one day. It is there that Fergus thought that Cuchulainn was, in Delga.

'I see a man coming towards us,' said Loeg to Cuchulainn. 'He has a yellow head of hair, and a linen emblem round it; a club of fury(?) in his hand, an ivory-hilted sword at his waist; a hooded tunic with red ornamentation on him.'

'Which of the warriors of the king is that?' said Cuchulainn.

Mac Roth asked Loeg whose man he was.

'Vassal to the man down yonder,' said Loeg.

Cuchulainn was there in the snow up to his two thighs, without anything at all on him, examining his shirt.

Then Mac Roth asked Cuchulainn whose man he was.

'Vassal of Conchobar Mac Nessa,' said Cuchulainn.

'Is there no clearer description?'

'That is enough,' said Cuchulainn.

'Where then is Cuchulainn?' said Mac Roth.

'What would you say to him?' said Cuchulainn.

Mac Roth tells him then all the message, as we have told it.

'Though Cuchulainn were near, he would not do this; he will not barter the brother of his mother for another king.'

He came to him again, and it was said to Cuchulainn that there should be given over to him the noblest of the women and the cows that were without milk, on condition that he should not ply his sling on them at night, even if he should kill them by day.

'I will not do it,' said Cuchulainn; 'if our slavewomen are taken from us, our noble women will be at the querns; and we shall be without milk if our milch-cows are taken from us.'

He came to him again, and he was told that he should have the slave-women and the milch-cows.

'I will not do it,' said Cuchulainn; 'the Ulstermen will take their slave-women to their beds, and there will be born to them a servile offspring, and they will use their milch-cows for meat in the winter.'

'Is there anything else then?' said the messenger.

'There is,' said Cuchulainn; 'and I will not tell it you. It shall be agreed to, if any one tell it you.'

'I know it,' said Fergus; 'I know what the man tried to suggest; and it is no advantage to you. And this is the agreement,' said Fergus: 'that the ford on which takes place (?) his battle and combat with one man, the cattle shall not be taken thence a day and a night; if perchance there come to him the help of the Ulstermen. And it is a marvel to me,' said Fergus, 'that it is so long till they come out of their sufferings.'

'It is indeed easier for us,' said Ailill, 'a man every day than a hundred every night.'

The Death of Etarcomol

Then Fergus went on this errand; Etarcomol, son of Edan [Note: Name uncertain. YBL has Eda, LL Feda.] and Lethrinne, foster-son of Ailill and Medb, followed.

'I do not want you to go,' said Fergus, 'and it is not for hatred of you; but I do not like combat between you and Cuchulainn. Your pride and insolence, and the fierceness and hatred, pride and madness of the other, Cuchulainn: there will be no good from your meeting.'

'Are you not able to protect me from him?' said Etarcomol.

'I can,' said Fergus, 'provided only that you do not treat his, sayings with disrespect.'

They go thence in two chariots to Delga. Cuchulainn was then playing chess [Note: *Buanfach*, like *fidchell*, is apparently a game something like chess or draughts.] with Loeg; the back of his head was towards them, and Loeg's face.

'I see two chariots coming towards us,' said Loeg; 'a great dark man in the first chariot, with dark and bushy hair; a purple cloak round him, and a golden pin therein; a hooded tunic with gold embroidery on him; and a round shield with an engraved edge of white metal, and a broad spear-head, with rings from point to haft(?), in his hand. A sword as long as the rudder of a boat on his two thighs.'

'It is empty, this great rudder that is brought by my friend Fergus,' said Cuchulainn; 'for there is no sword in its sheath except a sword of wood. It has been told to me,' said Cuchulainn; 'Ailill got a chance of them as they slept, he and Medb; and he took away his sword from Fergus, and gave it to his charioteer to take care of, and the sword of wood was put into its sheath.'

Then Fergus comes up.

'Welcome, O friend Fergus,' said Cuchulainn; 'if a fish comes into the estuary, you shall have it with half of another; if a flock comes into the plain, you shall have a duck with half of another; a spray of cress or seaweed, a spray of marshwort; a drink from the sand; you shall have a going to the ford to meet a man, if it should happen to be your watch, till you have slept.'

'I believe it,' said Fergus; 'it is not your provision that we have come for; we know your housekeeping here.'

Then Cuchulainn receives the message from Fergus; anti Fergus goes away. Etarcomol remains looking at Cuchulainn.

'What are you looking at?' said Cuchulainn.

'You,' said Etarcomol.

'The eye soon compasses it indeed,' said Cuchulainn.

'That is what I see,' said Etarcomol. 'I do not know at all why you should be feared by any one. I do not see terror or fearfulness, or overwhelming of a host, in you; you are merely a fair youth with arms of wood, and with fine feats.'

'Though you speak ill of me,' said Cuchulainn, 'I will not kill you for the sake of Fergus. But for your protection, it would have been your entrails drawn (?) and your quarters scattered, that would have gone from me to the camp behind your chariot.'

'Threaten me not thus,' said Etarcomol. 'The wonderful agreement that he has bound, that is, the single combat, it is I who will first meet you of the men of Ireland to-morrow.'

Then he goes away. He turned back from Methe and Cethe and said to his charioteer:

'I have boasted,' said he, 'before Fergus combat with Cuchulainn to-morrow. It is not possible for us [Note: YBL reading.] to wait for it; turn the horses back again from the hill.'

Loeg sees this and says to Cuchulainn: 'There is the chariot back again, and it has put its left board [Note: An insult.] towards us.'

'It is not a "debt of refusal,"' said Cuchulainn. 'I do not wish,' said Cuchulainn, 'what you demand of me.'

'This is obligatory to you,' said Etarcomol.

Cuchulainn strikes the sod under his feet, so that he fell prostrate, and the sod behind him.

'Go from me,' said Cuchulainn. 'I am loath to cleanse my hands in you. I would have divided you into many parts long since but for Fergus.'

'We will not part thus,' said Etarcomol, 'till I have taken your head, or left my head with you.'

'It is that indeed that will be there,' said Cuchulainn.

Cuchulainn strikes him with his sword in his two armpits, so that his clothes fell from him, and it did not wound his skin.

'Go then,' said Cuchulainn.

'No,' said Etarcomol.

Then Cuchulainn attacked him with the edge of his sword, and took his hair off as if it was shaved with a razor; he did not put even a scratch (?) on the surface. When the churl was troublesome then and stuck to him, he struck him on the hard part of his crown, so that he divided him down to the navel.

Fergus saw the chariot go past him, and the one man therein. He turned to quarrel with Cuchulainn.

'Ill done of you, O wild boy!' said he, 'to insult me. You would think my club [Note: Or 'track'?] short,' said he.

'Be not angry with me, O friend Fergus,' said Cuchulainn ... [Note: Rhetoric, five lines.] 'Reproach me not, O friend Fergus.'

He stoops down, so that Fergus's chariot went past him thrice.

He asked his charioteer: 'Is it I who have caused it?'

'It is not you at all,' said his charioteer.

'He said,' said Cuchulainn, 'he would not go till he took my head, or till he left his head with me. Which would you think easier to bear, O friend Fergus?' said

Cuchulainn.

'I think what has been done the easier truly,' said Fergus, 'for it is he who was insolent.'

Then Fergus put a spancel-withe through Etarcomol's two heels and took him behind his own chariot to the camp. When they went over rocks, one-half would separate from the other; when it was smooth, they came together again.

Medb saw him. 'Not pleasing is that treatment of a tender whelp, O Fergus,' said Medb.

'The dark churl should not have made fight,' said Fergus, 'against the great Hound whom he could not contend with (?).'

His grave is dug then and his stone planted; his name is written in ogam; his lament is celebrated. Cuchulainn did not molest them that night with his sling; and the women and maidens and half the cattle are taken to him; and provision continued to be brought to him by day.

The Death of Nadcrantail

'What man have you to meet Cuchulainn tomorrow?' said Lugaid.

'They will give it to you to-morrow,' said Mane, son of Ailill.

'We can find no one to meet him,' said Medb. 'Let us have peace with him till a man be sought for him.'

They get that then.

'Whither will you send,' said Ailill, 'to seek that man to meet Cuchulainn?'

'There is no one in Ireland who could be got for him,' said Medb, 'unless Curoi Mac Dare can be brought, or Nadcrantail the warrior.'

There was one of Curoi's followers in the tent. 'Curoi will not come,' said he; 'he thinks enough of his household has come. Let a message be sent to Nadcrantail.'

Mane Andoi goes to him, and they tell their tale to him.

'Come with us for the sake of the honour of Connaught.'

'I will not go,' said he, 'unless Findabair be given to me.'

He comes with them then. They bring his armour in a chariot, from the east of Connaught till it was in the camp.

'You shall have Findabair,' said Medb, 'for going against that man yonder.'

'I will do it,' said he.

Lugaid comes to Cuchulainn that night.

'Nadcrantail is coming to meet you to-morrow; it is unlucky for you: you will not withstand him.'

'That does not matter,' said Cuchulainn. ... [Note: Corrupt.]

Nadcrantail goes next morning from the camp, and he takes nine spits of holly, sharpened and burned. Now Cuchulainn was there catching birds, and his chariot near him. Nadcrantail throws a spear at Cuchulainn; Cuchulainn performed a feat on to the point of that spear, and it did not hinder him from catching the birds. The same with the eight other spears. When he throws the ninth spear, the flock flies from Cuchulainn, and he went after the flock. He goes on the points of the spears like a bird, from each spear to the next, pursuing the birds that they should not escape. It seemed to every one, however, that it was in flight that Cuchulainn went before Nadcrantail.

'Your Cuchulainn yonder,' said he, 'has gone in flight before me.'

'That is of course,' said Medb; 'if good warriors should come to him, the wild boy would not resist ----.'

This vexed Fergus and the Ulstermen; Fiacha Mac Fir-Febe comes from them to remonstrate with Cuchulainn.

'Tell him,' said Fergus, 'it was noble to be before the warriors while he did brave deeds. It is more noble for him,' said Fergus, 'to hide himself when he flees before one man, for it were not greater shame to him than to the rest of Ulster.'

'Who has boasted that?' said Cuchulainn.

'Nadcrantail,' said Fiacha.

'Though it were that that he should boast, the feat that I have done before him, it was no more shame to me,' (?) said Cuchulainn. 'He would by no means have boasted it had there been a weapon in his hand. You know full well that I kill no one unarmed. Let him come to-morrow,' said Cuchulainn, 'till he is between Ochaine and the sea, and however early he comes, he will find me there, and I shall not flee before him.'

Cuchulainn came then to his appointed meeting-place, and he threw the hem [of his cloak] round him after his night-watch, and he did not perceive the pillar that was near him, of equal size with himself. He embraced it under his cloak, and placed it near him.

Therewith Nadcrantail came; his arms were brought with him in a wagon.

'Where is Cuchulainn?' said he.

'There he is yonder,' said Fergus.

'It was not thus he appeared to me yesterday,' said Nadcrantail.

'Are you Cuchulainn?'

'And if I am then?' said Cuchulainn.

'If you are indeed,' said Nadcrantail, 'I cannot bring the head of a little lamb to camp; I will not take the head of a beardless boy.'

'It is not I at all,' said Cuchulainn. 'Go to him round the hill.'

Cuchulainn comes to Loeg: 'Smear a false beard on me,' said he; 'I cannot get the warrior to fight me without a beard.' It was done for him. He goes to meet him on the hill. 'I think that more fitting,' said he.

'Take the right way of fighting with me,' said Nadcrantail.

'You shall have it if only we know it,' said Cuchulainn.

'I will throw a cast at you,' said Nadcrantail, 'and do not avoid it.'

'I will not avoid it except on high,' said Cuchulainn.

Nadcrantail throws a cast at him; Cuchulainn leaps on high before it.

'You do ill to avoid my cast,' said Nadcrantail.

'Avoid my throw then on high,' said Cuchulainn.

Cuchulainn throws the spear at him, but it was on high, so that from above it alighted in his crown, and it went through him to the ground.

'Alas! it is you are the best warrior in Ireland!' said Nadcrantail. 'I have twenty-four sons in the camp. I will go and tell them what hidden treasures I have, and I will come that you may behead me, for I shall die if the spear is taken out of my head.'

'Good,' said Cuchulainn. 'You will come back.'

Nadcrantail goes to the camp then. Every one comes to meet him.

'Where is the madman's head?' said every one.

'Wait, O heroes, till I tell my tale to my sons, and go back that I may fight with Cuchulainn.'

He goes thence to seek Cuchulainn, and throws his sword at Cuchulainn. Cuchulainn leaps on high, so that it struck the pillar, and the sword broke in two. Then Cuchulainn went mad as he had done against the boys in Emain, and he springs on his shield therewith, and struck his head off. He strikes him again on the neck down to the navel. His four quarters fall to the ground. Then Cuchulainn said this:

'If Nadcrantail has fallen,
It will be an increase to the strife.
Alas! that I cannot fight at this time
With Medb with a third of the host.'

HERE IS THE FINDING OF THE BULL ACCORDING TO THIS VERSION:
It is then that Medb went with a third of the host with her to Cuib to seek the Bull; and Cuchulainn went after her. Now on the road of Midluachair she had gone to harry Ulster and Cruthne as far as Dun Sobairche. Cuchulainn saw something: Bude Mac Bain from Sliab Culinn with the Bull, and fifteen heifers round him; and his force was sixty men of Ailill's household, with a cloak folded round every man. Cuchulainn comes to them.

'Whence have you brought the cattle?' said Cuchulainn.

'From the mountain yonder,' said the man.'

'Where are their cow-herds?' said Cuchulainn.

'He is as we found him,' said the man.

Cuchulainn made three leaps after them to seek speech with them as far as the ford. It is there he said to the leader:

'What is your name?' said he.

'One who fears you not(?) and loves you not; Bude Mac Bain,' said he.

'This spear at Bude!' said Cuchulainn. He hurls at him the javelin, so that it went through his armpits, and one of the livers broke in two before the spear. He kills him on his ford; hence is Ath Bude. The Bull is brought into the camp then. They considered then that it would not be difficult to deal with Cuchulainn, provided his javelin were got from him.

The Death of Redg the Satirist
It is then that Redg, Ailill's satirist, went to him on an errand to seek the javelin, that is, Cuchulainn's spear.

'Give me your spear,' said the satirist.

'Not so,' said Cuchulainn; 'but I will give you treasure.'

'I will not take it,' said the satirist.

Then Cuchulainn wounded the satirist, because he would not accept from him what he offered him, and the satirist said he would take away his honour unless he got the javelin. Then Cuchulainn threw the javelin at him, and it went right through his head.

'This gift is overpowering (?),' said the satirist. Hence is Ath Tolam Set.

There was now a ford east of it, where the copper of the javelin rested; Humarrith, then, is the name of that ford. It is there that Cuchulainn killed all those that we have mentioned in Cuib; i.e. Nathcoirpthe at his trees; Cruthen on his ford; the sons of the Herd at their cairn; Marc on his hill; Meille on his hill; Bodb in his tower; Bogaine in his marsh (?).

Cuchulainn turned back to Mag Murthemne; he liked better to defend his own home. After he went, he killed the men of Crocen (or Cronech), i.e. Focherd; twenty men of Focherd. He overtook them taking camp: ten cup-bearers and ten fighting-men.

Medb turned back from the north when she had remained a fortnight ravaging the province, and when she had fought a battle against Findmor, wife of Celtchar Mac Uthidir. And after taking Dun Sobairche upon her, she brought fifty women into the province of Dalriada. Wherever Medb placed a horse-switch in Cuib its name is Bile Medba [Note: i.e. Tree of Medb]; every ford and every hill by which she slept, its name is Ath Medba and Dindgna Medba.

They all meet then at Focherd, both Ailill and Medb and the troop that drove the Bull. But their herd took their Bull from them, and they drove him across into a narrow gap with their spear-shafts on their shields(?). [Note: A very doubtful rendering.] So that the feet of the cattle drove him [Note, i.e. Forgemen.] through the ground. Forgemen was the herd's name. He is there afterwards, so that that is the name of the hill, Forgemen. There was no annoyance to them that night, provided a man were got toward off Cuchulainn on the ford.

'Let a sword-truce be asked by us from Cuchulainn,' said Ailill.

'Let Lugaid go for it,' said every one.

Lugaid goes then to speak to him.

'How am I now with the host?' said Cuchulainn.

'Great indeed is the mockery that you asked of them,' said Lugaid, 'that is, your women and your maidens and half your cattle. And they think it heavier than anything to be killed and to provide you with food.'

A man fell there by Cuchulainn every day to the end of a week. Fair-play is broken with Cuchulainn: twenty are sent to attack him at one time; and he killed them all.

'Go to him, O Fergus,' said Ailill, 'that he may allow us a change of place.'

They go then to Cronech. This is what fell by him in single combat at this place: two Roths, two Luans, two female horse messengers, [Note: Or 'female stealers.' (O'Davoren.)] ten fools, ten cup-bearers, ten Ferguses, six Fedelms, six Fiachras. These then were all killed by him in single combat. When they pitched their tents in Cronech, they considered what they should do against Cuchulainn.

'I know,' said Medb, 'what is good in this case: let a message be sent from us to ask him that we may have a sword-truce from him towards the host, and he shall have half the cattle that are here.'

This message is taken to him.

'I will do this,' said Cuchulainn, 'provided the compact is not broken by you.'

The Meeting of Cuchulainn and Findabair

'Let an offer go to him,' said Ailill, 'that Findabair will be given to him on condition that he keeps away from the hosts.'

Mane Athramail goes to him. He goes first to Loeg.

'Whose man are you?' said he.

Loeg does not speak to him. Mane spoke to him thrice in this way.

'Cuchulainn's man,' said he, 'and do not disturb me, lest I strike your head off.'

'This man is fierce,' said Mane, turning from him. He goes then to speak to Cuchulainn. Now Cuchulainn had taken off his tunic, and the snow was round him up to his waist as he sat, and the snow melted round him a cubit for the greatness of the heat of the hero.

Mane said to him in the same way thrice, 'whose man was he?'

'Conchobar's man, and do not disturb me. If you disturb me any longer, I will strike your head from you as the head is taken from a blackbird.'

'It is not easy,' said Mane, 'to speak to these two.'

Mane goes from them then and tells his tale to Ailill and Medb.

'Let Lugaid go to him,' said Ailill, 'and offer to him the maiden.'

Lugaid goes then and tells Cuchulainn that.

'O friend Lugaid,' said Cuchulainn, 'this is a snare.'

'It is the king's word that has said it,' said Lugaid; 'there will be no snare there-from.'

'Let it be done so,' said Cuchulainn.

Lugaid went from him therewith, and tells Ailill and Medb that answer.

'Let the fool go in my form,' said Ailill, 'and a king's crown on his head, and let him stand at a distance from Cuchulainn lest he recognise him, and let the maiden go with him, and let him betroth her to him, and let them depart quickly in this way; and it is likely that you will play a trick on him thus, so that he will not hinder you, till he comes with the Ulstermen to the battle.'

Then the fool goes to him, and the maiden also; and it was from a distance he spoke to Cuchulainn. Cuchulainn goes to meet them. It happened that he recognised by the man's speech that he was a fool. He threw a sling stone that was in his hand at him, so that it sprang into his head and brought his brains out. Then he comes to the maiden, cuts her two tresses off, and thrusts a stone through her mantle and through her tunic, and thrusts a stone pillar through the middle of the fool. There are their two pillars there: the pillar of Findabair, and the fool's pillar.

Cuchulainn left them thus. A party was sent from Ailill and Medb to seek out their folk, for they thought they were long; they were seen in this position. All this was heard throughout the camp. There was no truce for them with Cuchulainn afterwards.

The Combat of Munremar and Curoi

When the hosts were there in the evening; they saw that one stone lighted on them from the east, and another from the west to meet it. They met in the air, and kept falling between Fergus's camp, and Ailill's, and Era's. [Note: Or Nera?] This sport and play went on from that hour to the same hour next day; and the hosts were sitting down, and their shields were over their heads to protect them against the masses of stones, till the plain was full of the stones. Hence is Mag Clochair. It happened that Curoi Mac Daire did this; he had come to help his comrades, and he was in Cotal over against Munremar Mac Gerrcind. He had come from Emain Macha to help Cuchulainn, and he was in Ard Roich. Curoi knew that there was no man in the host who could withstand Munremar. So it was these two who had made this sport between them. They were asked by the host to be quiet; then Munremar and Curoi make peace, and Curoi goes to his house and Munremar to Emain Macha. And Munremar did not come till the day of the battle; Curoi did not come till the combat with Fer Diad.

'Speak to Cuchulainn,' said Medb and Ailill, 'that he allow us change of place.'

It is granted to them then, and they change the place. The weakness of the Ulstermen was over then. For when they awoke from their suffering, some of them kept coming on the host, that they might take to slaying them again.

The Death of the Boys

Then the boys of Ulster had consulted in Emain Macha.

'Wretched indeed,' said they, 'for our friend Cuchulainn to be without help.'

'A question indeed,' said Fiachna Fulech Mac Fir-Febe, own brother to Fiacha Fialdama Mac Fir-Febe, 'shall I have a troop among you, and go to take help to him therefrom?'

Three fifties of boys go with their playing-clubs, and that was a third of the boys of Ulster. The host saw them coming towards them across the plain.

'A great host is at hand to us over the plain,' said Ailill.

Fergus goes to look at them. 'Some of the boys of Ulster that,' said he; 'and they come to Cuchulainn's help.'

'Let a troop go against them,' said Ailill, 'without Cuchulainn's knowledge; for if they meet him, you will not withstand them.'

Three fifties of warriors go to meet them. They fell by one another so that no one escaped alive of the abundance(?) of the boys at Lia Toll. Hence it is the Stone of Fiachra Mac Fir-Febe; for it is there he fell.

'Make a plan,' said Ailill.

'Ask Cuchulainn about letting you go out of this place, for you will not come beyond him by force, because his flame of valour has sprung.'

For it was customary with him, when his flame of valour sprang in him, that his feet would go round behind him, and his hams before; and the balls of his calves on his shins, and one eye in his head and the other out of his head; a man's head could have gone into his mouth. Every hair on him was as sharp as a thorn of hawthorn, and a drop of blood on each hair. He would not recognise comrades or friends. He would strike alike before and behind. It is from this that the men of Connaught gave Cuchulainn the name Riastartha.

The Woman-fight of Rochad

Cuchulainn sent his charioteer to Rochad Mac Fatheman of Ulster, that he should come to his help. Now it happened that Findabair loved Rochad, for he was the fairest of the warriors among the Ulstermen at that time. The man goes to Rochad and told him to come to help Cuchulainn if he had come out of his weakness; that they should deceive the host, to get at some of them to slay them. Rochad comes from the north with a hundred men.

'Look at the plain for us to-day,' said Ailill.

'I see a troop coming over the plain,' said the watchman, 'and a warrior of tender years among them; the men only reach up to his shoulders.'

'Who is it yonder, O Fergus?' said Ailill.

'Rochad Mac Fatheman,' said he, 'and it is to help Cuchulainn he comes.'

'I know what you had better do with him,' said Fergus. 'Let a hundred men go from you with the maiden yonder to the middle of the plain, and let the maiden go before them; and let a horseman go to speak to him, that he come alone to speak with the maiden, and let hands be laid on him, and this will keep off (?) the attack of his army from us.'

This is done then. Rochad goes to meet the horseman.

'I have come from Findabair to meet you, that you come to speak with her.'

He goes then to speak with her alone. The host rushes about him from every side. He is taken, and hands are laid on him. His force breaks into flight. He is let go then, and he is bound over not to go against the host till he should come together with all Ulster. It was promised to him that Findabair should be given to him, and he returned from them then. So that that is Rochad's Woman-fight.

The Death of the Princes [Note: Or 'royal mercenaries.']

'Let a sword-truce be asked of Cuchulainn for us,' said Ailill and Medb.

Lugaid goes on that errand, and Cuchulainn grants the truce.

'Put a man on the ford for me to-morrow,' said Cuchulainn.

There were with Medb six princes, i.e. six king's heirs of the Clanna Dedad, the three Blacks of Imlech, and the three Reds of Sruthair.

'Why should we not go against Cuchulainn?' said they.

They go next day, and Cuchulainn slew the six of them.

The Death of Cur

Then Cur Mac Dalath is besought to go against Cuchulainn. He from whom he shed blood, he is dead before the ninth day.

'If he slay him,' said Medb, 'it is victory; and though it be he who is slain, it is removing a load from the host: for it is not easy to be with him in regard to eating and sleeping.'

Then he goes forth. He did not think it good to go against a beardless wild boy.

'Not so(?) indeed,' said he, 'right is the honour (?) that you give us! If I had known that it was against this man that I was sent, I would not have bestirred myself to seek him; it were enough in my opinion for a boy of his own age from my troop to go against him.'

'Not so,' said Cormac Condlongas; 'it were a marvel for us if you yourself were to drive him off.'

'Howbeit,' said he, 'since it is on myself that it is laid you Shall go forth tomorrow morning; it will not delay me to kill the young deer yonder.'

He goes then early in the morning to meet him; and he tells the host to get ready to take the road before them, for it was a clear road that he would make by going against Cuchulainn.

This is the Number of the Feats

He went on that errand then. Cuchulainn was practising feats at that time, i.e. the apple-feat, the edge-feat, the supine-feat, the javelin-feat, the ropefeat, the ---- feat, the cat-feat, the hero's salmon[-leap?], the cast ----, the leap over ----, the noble champion's turn, the *gae bolga*, the ---- of swiftness, the wheel-feat, the ----, the feat on breath, the mouth-rage (?), the champion's shout, the stroke with proper adjustment, the back-stroke, the climbing a javelin with stretching of the body on its point, with the binding (?) of a noble warrior.

Cur was plying his weapons against him in a fence(?) of his shield till a third of the day; and not a stroke of the blow reached Cuchulainn for the madness of the feats, and he did not know that a man was trying to strike him, till Fiacha Mac Fir-Febe said to him: 'Beware of the man who is attacking you.'

Cuchulainn looked at him; he threw the feat-apple that remained in his hand, so that it went between the rim and the body of the shield, and went back through the head of the churl. It would be in Imslige Glendanach that Cur fell according to another version.

Fergus returned to the army. 'If your security hold you,' said he, 'wait here till to-morrow.'

'It would not be there,' said Ailill; 'we shall go back to our camp.'

Then Lath Mac Dabro is asked to go against Cuchulainn, as Cur had been asked. He himself fell then also. Fergus returns again to put his security on them. They remained there until there were slain there Cur Mac Dalath, and Lath Mac Dabro, and Foirc, son of the three Swifts, and Srubgaile Mac Eobith. They were all slain there in single combat.

The Death of Ferbaeth

'Go to the camp for us, O friend Loeg' [said Cuchulainn], 'and consult Lugaid Mac Nois, descendant of Lomarc, to know who is coming against me tomorrow. Let it be asked diligently, and give him my greeting.'

Then Loeg went.

'Welcome,' said Lugaid; 'it is unlucky for Cuchulainn, the trouble in which he is, alone against the men of Ireland. It is a comrade of us both, Ferbaeth (ill-luck to his arms!), who goes against him to morrow. Findabair is given to him for it, and the kingdom of his race.'

Loeg turns back to where Cuchulainn is.

He is not very joyful over his answer, my friend Loeg,' said Cuchulainn.

Loeg tells him all that. Ferbaeth had been summoned into the tent to Ailill and Medb, and he is told to sit by Findabair, and that she should be given to him, for he was her choice for fighting with Cuchulainn. He was the man they thought worthy of them, for they had both learned the same arts with Scathach. Then wine is given to him, till he was intoxicated, and he is told, 'They thought that wine fine, and there had only been brought the load of fifty wagons. And it was the maiden who used to put hand to his portion therefrom.'

'I do not wish it,' said Ferbaeth; 'Cuchulainn is my foster-brother, and a man of perpetual covenant with me. Nevertheless I will go against him to-morrow and cut off his head.'

'It will be you who would do it,' said Medb.

Cuchulainn told Loeg to go to meet Lugaid, that he should come and speak with him. Lugaid comes to him.

'So Ferbaeth is coming against me to-morrow,' said Cuchulainn.

'He indeed,' said Lugaid.

'An evil day!' said Cuchulainn; 'I shall not be alive therefrom. Two of equal age we, two of equal deftness, two equal when we meet. O Lugaid, greet him for me; tell him that it is not true valour to come against me; tell him to come to meet me to-night, to speak with me.'

Lugaid tells him this. When Ferbaeth did not avoid it, he went that night to renounce his friendship with Cuchulainn, and Fiacha Mac Fir-Febe with him. Cuchulainn appealed to him by his foster-brotherhood, and Scathach, the foster-mother of them both.

'I must,' said Ferbaeth. 'I have promised it'

'Take back (?) your bond of friendship then,' said Cuchulainn.

Cuchulainn went from him in anger. A spear of holly was driven into Cuchulainn's foot in the glen, and appeared up by his knee. He draws it out.

'Go not, O Ferbaeth, till you have seen the find that I have found.'

'Throw it,' said Ferbaeth.

Cuchulainn threw the spear then after Ferbaeth so that it hit the hollow of his poll, and came out at his mouth in front, so that he fell back into the glen.

'That is a throw indeed,' said Ferbaeth. Hence is Focherd Murthemne. (Or it is Fiacha who had said, 'Your throw is vigorous to-day, O Cuchulainn,' said he; so that Focherd Murthemne is from that.)

Ferbaeth died at once in the glen. Hence is Glenn Firbaith. Something was heard: Fergus, who said:

'O Ferbaeth, foolish is thy expedition
In the place in which thy grave is.
Ruin reached thee ...
In Croen Corand.

'The hill is named Fithi (?) for ever;
Croenech in Murthemne,
From to-day Focherd will be the name
Of the place in which thou didst fall, O Ferbaeth.
O Ferbaeth,' etc.

'Your comrade has fallen,' said Fergus. 'Say will you pay for this man on the morrow?'

'I will pay indeed,' said Cuchulainn.

Cuchulainn sends Loeg again for news, to know how they are in the camp, and whether Ferbaeth lived. Lugaid said: 'Ferbaeth is dead,' and Cuchulainn comes in turn to talk with them.

The Combat of Larine Mac Nois

'One of you to-morrow to go readily against the other,' said Lugaid.

'He will not be found at all,' said Ailill, 'unless you practise trickery therein. Any man who comes to you, give him wine, so that his mind may be glad, and it shall be said to him that that is all the wine that has been brought from Cruachan. It grieves us that you should be on water in the camp. And Findabair shall be put at his right hand, and it shall be said: "She shall come to you, if you bring us the head of the Riastartha."'

A messenger used to be sent to every hero on his night, and that used to be told to him; he continued to kill every man of them in. turn. No one could be got by them to meet him at last. Larine Mac Nois, brother to Lugaid, King of Munster, was summoned to them the next day. Great was his pride. Wine is given to him, and Findabair is put at his right hand.

Medb looked at the two. 'It pleases me, yonder pair,' said she; 'a match between them would be fitting.'

'I will not stand in your way,' said Ailill; 'he shall have her if he brings me the head of the Riastartha.'

'I will bring it,' said Larine.

Then Lugaid comes. 'What man have you for the ford to-morrow?' said he.

'Larine goes,' said Ailill.

Then Lugaid comes to speak with Cuchulainn. They meet in Glenn Firbaith. Each gives the other welcome.

'It is for this I have come to speak to you,' said Lugaid: 'there is a churl here, a fool and proud,' said he, 'a brother of mine named Larine; he is befooled about the same maiden. On your friendship then, do not kill him, lest you should leave me without a brother. For it is for this that he is being sent to you, so that we two might quarrel. I should be content, however, that you should give him a sound drubbing, for it is in my despite that he comes.'

Larine goes next day to meet Cuchulainn, and the maiden near him to encourage him. Cuchulainn attacks him without arms. [Note: This is apparently the sense, but the passage seems corrupt.] He takes Larine's arms from him perforce. He takes him then between his two hands, and grinds and shakes him, ... and threw him till he was between Lugaid's two hands ...; nevertheless, he is the only man who escaped [even] a bad escape from him, of all who met him on the Tain.

The Conversation of the Morrigan with Cuchulainn

Cuchulainn saw a young woman coming towards him, with a dress of every colour on, and her form very excellent.

'Who are you?' said Cuchulainn.

'Daughter of Buan the king,' said she. 'I have come to you; I have loved you for your reputation, and I have brought my treasures and my cattle with me.'

'The time at which you have come to us is not good. For our condition is evil, through hunger. It is not easy to me to meet a woman, while I am in this strife.'

'I will be a help to you. ... I shall be more troublesome to you,' said she, 'when I come against you when you are in combat against the men. I will come in the form of an eel about your feet in the ford, so that you shall fall.'

'I think that likelier than the daughter of a king. I will take you,' said he, 'between my toes, till your ribs are broken, and you will be in this condition till a doom of blessing comes (?) on you.'

'I will drive the cattle on the ford to you, in the form of a grey she-wolf.'

'I will throw a stone at you from my sling, so that it shall break your eye in your head; and you will be in that state till a doom of blessing comes on you.'

'I will come to you in the form of a hornless red heifer before the cattle. They will rush on you on the plains(?), and on the fords, and on the pools, and you will not see me before you.'

'I will throw a stone at you,' said he, 'so that your leg shall break under you, and you will be in this state till a doom of blessing comes on you.'

Therewith she goes from him.

So he was a week on Ath Grencha, and a man used to fall every day by him in Ath Grencha, i.e. in Ath Darteisc.

The Death of Loch Mac Emonis

Then Loch Mac Emonis was asked like the others, and there was promised to him a piece of the arable land of Mag Ai equal in size to Mag Murthemne, and the equipment of twelve warriors and a chariot worth seven cumals [Note: A measure of value.]; and he did not think combat with a youth worthy. He had a brother, Long Mac Emonis himself. The same price was given to him, both maiden and raiment and chariots and land. He goes to meet Cuchulainn. Cuchulainn slays him, and he was brought dead before his brother, Loch.

This latter said that if he only knew that it was a bearded man who slew him, he would kill him for it.

'Take a battle-force to him,' said Medb to her household, 'across the ford from the west, that you may go-across; and let fair-play be broken on him.'

Then the seven Manes, warriors, go first, so that they saw him on the edge of the ford westward. He puts his feast-dress on that day. It is then that the women kept climbing on the men to look at him.

'I am sorry,' said Medb; 'I cannot see the boy about whom they go there.'

'Your mind will not be the gladder for it,' said Lethrend, Ailill's squire, 'if you could see him.'

He comes to the ford then as he was.

'What man is it yonder, O Fergus?' said Medb.

'A boy who wards off,' etc. ... 'if it is Culann's Hound.' [Note: Rhetoric, four lines.]

Medb climbed on the men then to look at him.

It is then that the women said to Cuchulainn 'that he was laughed at in the camp because he had no beard, and no good warriors would go against him, only wild men; it were easier to make a false beard.' So this is what he did, in order to seek combat with a man; i.e. with Loch. Cuchulainn took a handful of grass, and said a spell over it, so that every one thought he had a beard.

'True,' said the troop of women, 'Cuchulainn has a beard. It is fitting for a warrior to fight with him.'

They had done this on urging Loch.

'I will not make combat against him till the end of seven days from to-day,' said Loch.

'It is not fitting for us to have no attack on the man for this space,' said Medb.

'Let us put a hero to hunt(?) him every night, if perchance we may get a chance at him.'

This is done then. A hero used to come every night to hunt him, and he used to kill them all. These are the names of the men who fell there: seven Conalls, seven Oenguses, seven Uarguses, seven Celtris, eight Fiacs, ten Ailills, ten Delbaths, ten Tasachs. These are his deeds of this week in Ath Grencha.

Medb asked advice, to know what she should do to Cuchulainn, for what had been killed of their hosts by him distressed her greatly. This is the plan she arrived at, to put brave, high-spirited men to attack him all at once when he should come to an appointed meeting to speak with Medb. For she had an appointment the next day with Cuchulainn to make a peace in fraud with him, to get hold of him. She sent messengers forth to seek him that he should come to meet her; and it was thus he should come, and he unarmed: 'for she would come only with her troop of women to meet him.'

The messenger, Traigtren, went to the place where Cuchulainn was, and tells him Medb's message. Cuchulainn promised that he would do so.

'In what manner does it please you to go to meet Medb to-morrow, O Cuchulainn?' said Loeg.

'As Medb has asked me,' said Cuchulainn.

'Great are Medb's deeds,' said the charioteer; 'I fear a hand behind the back with her.'

'How is it to be done then?' said he.

'Your sword at your waist,' said the charioteer, 'that you may not be taken at an unfair advantage. For the warrior is not entitled to his honour-price if he is without arms; and it is the coward's law that he deserves in that way.'

'Let it be done so then,' said Cuchulainn.

The meeting-place was in Ard Aignech, which is called Fochaird to-day. Now Medb came to the meeting-place and set in ambush fourteen men of her own special following, of those who were of most prowess, ready for him. These are they: two Glassines, the two sons of Bucchridi; two Ardans, the two sons of Licce; two Glasogmas, the two sons of Crund; Drucht and Delt and Dathen; Tea and Tascra and Tualang; Taur and Glese.

Then Cuchulainn comes to meet her. The men rise to attack him. Fourteen spears are thrown at him at once. Cuchulainn guards himself so that his skin or his ---- (?) is not touched. Then he turns on them and kills them, the fourteen of them. So that they are the fourteen men of Focherd, and they are the men of Cronech, for it is in Cronech at Focherd that they were killed. Hence Cuchulainn said: 'Good is my feat of heroism,' [Note: *Fo*, 'good'; *cherd*, 'feat.' Twelve lines of rhetoric.] etc.

So it is from this that the name Focherd stuck to the place; that is, *focherd*, i.e. 'good is the feat of arms' that happened to Cuchulainn there.

So Cuchulainn came, and overtook them taking camp, and there were slain two Daigris and two Anlis and four Dungais of Imlech. Then Medb began to urge Loch there.

'Great is the mockery of you,' said she, 'for the man who has killed your brother to be destroying our host, and you do not go to battle with him! For we deem it certain that the wild man, great and fierce [Note: Literally, 'sharpened.'], the like of him yonder, will not be able to withstand the rage and fury of a hero like you. For it is by one foster-mother and instructress that an art was built up for you both.'

Then Loch came against Cuchulainn, to avenge his brother on him, for it was shown to him that Cuchulainn had a beard.

'Come to the upper ford,' said Loch; 'it would not be in the polluted ford that we shall meet, where Long fell.'

When he came then to seek the ford, the men drove the cattle across.

'It will be across your water [Note: Irish, *tarteisc*.] here to-day,' said Gabran the poet. Hence is Ath Darteisc, and Tir Mor Darteisc from that time on this place.

When the men met then on the ford, and when they began to fight and to strike each other there, and when each of them began to strike the other, the eel threw three folds round Cuchulainn's feet, till he lay on his back athwart the ford. Loch attacked him with the sword, till the ford was blood-red with his blood.

'Ill indeed,' said Fergus, 'is this deed before the enemy. Let each of you taunt the man, O men,' said he to his following, 'that he may not fall for nothing.'

Bricriu Poison-tongue Mac Carbatha rose and began inciting Cuchulainn.

'Your strength is gone,' said he, 'when it is a little salmon that overthrows you when the Ulstermen are at hand [coming] to you out of their sickness yonder. Grievous for you to undertake a hero's deed in the presence of the men of Ireland and to ward off a formidable warrior in arms thus!'

Therewith Cuchulainn arises and strikes the eel so that its ribs broke in it, and the cattle were driven over the hosts eastwards by force, so that they took the tents on their horns, with the thunder-feat that the two heroes had made in the ford.

The she-wolf attacked him, and drove the cattle on him westwards. He throws a stone from his sling, so that her eye broke in her head. She goes in the form of a hornless red heifer; she rushes before the cows upon the pools and fords. It is then he said: 'I cannot see the fords for water.' He throws a stone at the hornless red heifer, so that her leg breaks under her. Then he sang a song:

'I am all alone before flocks;
I get them not, I let them not go;
I am alone at cold hours (?)
Before many peoples.

'Let some one say to Conchobar
Though he should come to me it were not too soon;
Magu's sons have carried off their kine
And divided them among them.

'There may be strife about one head
Only that one tree blazes not;
If there were two or three
Their brands would blaze. [Note: Meaning not clear.]

'The men have almost worn me out
By reason of the number of single combats;
I cannot work the slaughter (?) of glorious warriors
As I am all alone.
I am all alone.'

It is there then that Cuchulainn did to the Morrigan the three things that he had promised her in the *Tain Bo Regamna* [Note: One of the introductory stories to the *Tain Bo Cuailnge*, printed with translation in *Irische Texte*, 2nd series.];

and he fights Loch in the ford with the gae-bolga, which the charioteer threw him along the stream. He attacked him with it, so that it went into his body's armour, for Loch had a horn-skin in fighting with a man.

'Give way to me,' said Loch. Cuchulainn gave way, so that it was on the other side that Loch fell. Hence is Ath Traiged in Tir Mor. Cuchulainn cut off his head then.

Then fair-play was broken with him that day when five men came against him at one time; i.e. two Cruaids, two Calads, Derothor; Cuchulainn killed them by himself. Hence is Coicsius Focherda, and Coicer Oengoirt; or it is fifteen days that Cuchulainn was in Focherd, and hence is Coicsius Focherda in the Foray.

Cuchulainn hurled at them from Delga, so that not a living thing, man or beast, could put its head past him southwards between Delga and the sea.

The Healing of the Morrigan

When Cuchulainn was in this great weariness, the Morrigan met him in the form of an old hag, and she blind and lame, milking a cow with three teats, and he asked her for a drink. She gave him milk from a teat.

'He will be whole who has brought it(?),' said Cuchulainn; 'the blessings of gods and non-gods on you,' said he. (Gods with them were the Mighty Folk [Note: i.e. the dwellers in the Sid. The words in brackets are a gloss incorporated in the text.]; non-gods the people of husbandry.)

Then her head was healed so that it was whole.

She gave the milk of the second teat, and her eye was whole; and gave the milk of the third teat, and her leg was whole. So that this was what he said about each thing of them, 'A doom of blessing on you,' said he.

'You told me,' said the Morrigan, 'I should not have healing from you for ever.'

'If I had known it was you,' said Cuchulainn, 'I would not have healed you ever.'

So that formerly Cuchulainn's throng (?) on Tarthesc was the name of this story in the Foray.

It is there that Fergus claimed of his securities that faith should not be broken with Cuchulainn; and it is there that Cuchulainn ... [Note: Corrupt; one and a half lines.] i.e. Delga Murthemne at that time.

Then Cuchulainn killed Fota in his field; Bomailce on his ford; Salach in his village (?); Muine in his hill; Luair in Leth-bera; Fer-Toithle in Toithle; these are the names of these lands for ever, every place in which each man of them fell. Cuchulainn killed also Traig and Dornu and Dernu, Col and Mebul and Eraise on this side of Ath Tire Moir, at Methe and Cethe: these were three [Note: MS. 'two.'] druids and their three wives.

Then Medb sent a hundred men of her special retinue to kill Cuchulainn. . He killed them all on Ath Ceit-Chule. Then Medb said: 'It is *cuillend* [Note: Interlinear gloss: 'We deem it a crime.'] to us, the slaying of our people.' Hence is Glass Chrau and Cuillend Cind Duin and Ath Ceit-Chule.

Then the four provinces of Ireland took camp and fortified post in the Breslech Mor in Mag Murthemne, and send part of their cattle and booty beyond them to the south into Clithar Bo Ulad. Cuchulainn took his post at the mound in Lerga near them, and his charioteer Loeg Mac Riangabra kindled a fire for him on the evening of that night. He saw the fiery sheen of the bright golden arms over the heads of the four provinces of Ireland at the setting of the clouds of evening. Fury and great rage came over him at sight of the host, at the multitude of his enemies, the abundance of his foes. He took his two spears and his shield and his sword; he shook his shield and brandished his spears and waved his sword; and he uttered his hero's shout from his throat, so that goblins and sprites and spectres of the glen and demons of the air answered, for the terror of the shout which they uttered on high. So that the Nemain produced confusion on the host. The four provinces of Ireland came into a tumult of weapons about the points of their own spears and weapons, so that a hundred warriors of them died of terror and of heart-burst in the middle of the camp and of the position that night.

When Loeg was there, he saw something: a single man who came straight across the camp of the men of Ireland from the north-east straight towards him.

'A single man is coming to us now, O Little Hound!' said Loeg.

'What kind of man is there?' said Cuchulainn.

'An easy question: a man fair and tall is he, with hair cut broad, waving yellow hair; a green mantle folded round him; a brooch of white silver in the mantle on his breast; a tunic of royal silk, with red ornamentation of red gold against the white skin, to his knees. A black shield with a hard boss of white metal; a five pointed spear in his hand; a forked (?) javelin beside it. Wonderful is the play and sport and exercise that he makes; but no one attacks him, and he attacks no one, as if no one saw him.'

'It is true, O fosterling,' said he; 'which of my friends from the *sid* is that who comes to have pity on me, because they know the sore distress in which I am, alone against the four great provinces of Ireland, on the Cattle-Foray of Cualnge at this time?'

That was true for Cuchulainn. When the warrior had reached the place where Cuchulainn was, he spoke to him, and had pity on him for it.

'This is manly, O Cuchulainn,' said he.

'It is not much at all,' said Cuchulainn.

'I will help you,' said the man.

'Who are you at all?' said Cuchulainn.

'It is I, your father from the *sid*, Lug Mac Ethlend.'

'My wounds are heavy, it were high time that I should be healed.'

'Sleep a little, O Cuchulainn,' said the warrior; 'your heavy swoon (?) [Note: Conjectural--MS. *tromthortim*.] of sleep at the mound of Lerga till the end of three days and three nights, and I will fight against the hosts for that space.'

Then he sings the *ferdord* to him, and he sleeps from it. Lug looked at each wound that it was clean. Then Lug said:

'Arise, O great son of the Ulstermen, whole of thy wounds. ... Go into thy chariot secure. Arise, arise!' [Note: Rhetoric.]

For three days and three nights Cuchulainn was asleep. It were right indeed though his sleep equalled his weariness. From the Monday after the end of summer exactly to the Wednesday after Candlemas, for this space Cuchulainn had not slept, except when he slept a little while against his spear after midday, with his head on his clenched fist, and his clenched fist on his spear, and his spear on his knee; but he was striking and cutting and attacking and slaying the four great provinces of Ireland for that space.

It is then that the warrior of the sid cast herbs and grasses of curing and charms of healing into the hurts and wounds and into the injuries and into the many wounds of Cuchulainn, so that Cuchulainn recovered in his sleep without his perceiving it at all.

Now it was at this time that the boys came south from Emain Macha: Folloman Mac Conchobair with three fifties of kings' sons of Ulster, and they gave battle thrice to the hosts, so that three times their own number fell, and all the boys fell except Folloman Mac Conchobair. Folloman boasted that he would not go back to Emain for ever and ever, until he should take the head of Ailill with him, with the golden crown that was above it. This was not easy to him; for the two sons of Bethe Mac Bain, the two sons of Ailill's foster-mother and foster-father, came on him, and wounded him so that he fell by them. So that that is the death of the boys of Ulster and of Folloman Mac Conchobair.

Cuchulainn for his part was in his deep sleep till the end of three days and three nights at the mound in Lerga. Cuchulainn arose then from his sleep, and put his hand over his face, and made a purple wheelbeam from head to foot, and his mind was strong in him, and he would have gone to an assembly, or a march, or a tryst, or a beer-house, or to one of the chief assemblies of Ireland.

'How long have I been in this sleep now, O warrior?' said Cuchulainn.

'Three days and three nights,' said the warrior.

'Alas for that!' said Cuchulainn.

'What is the matter?' said the warrior.

'The hosts without attack for this space,' said Cuchulainn.

'They are not that at all indeed,' said the warrior.

'Who has come upon them?' said Cuchulainn.

'The boys came from the north from Emain Macha; Folloman Mac Conchobair with three fifties of boys of the kings' sons of Ulster; and they gave three battles to the hosts for the space of the three days and the three nights in which you have been in your sleep now. And three times their own number fell, and the boys fell, except Folloman Mac Conchobair. Folloman boasted that he would take Ailill's head, and that was not easy to him, for he was killed.'

'Pity for that, that I was not in my strength! For if I had been in my strength, the boys would not have fallen as they have fallen, and Folloman Mac Conchobair would not have fallen.'

'Strive further, O Little Hound, it is no reproach to thy honour and no disgrace to thy valour.'

'Stay here for us to-night, O warrior,' said Cuchulainn, 'that we may together avenge the boys on the hosts.'

'I will not stay indeed,' said the warrior, 'for however great the contests of valour and deeds of arms any one does near thee, it is not on him there will be the renown of it or the fame or the reputation, but it is on thee; therefore I will not stay. But ply thy deed of arms thyself alone on the hosts, for not with them is there power over thy life this time.'

'The scythe-chariot, O my friend Loeg!' said Cuchulainn; 'can you yoke it? and is its equipment here? If you can yoke it, and if you have its equipment, yoke it; and if you have not its equipment, do not yoke it at all.'

It is then that the charioteer arose, and he put on his hero's dress of charioteering. This was his hero's dress of charioteering that he put on: his soft tunic of skin, light and airy, well-turned [Note: Lit. 'kneaded.'], made of skin, sewn, of deer-skin, so that it did not restrain the movement of his hands outside. He put on his black (?) upper-cloak over it outside: Simon Magus had made it for Darius, King of the Romans, so that Darius gave it to Conchobar, and Conchobar gave it to Cuchulainn, and Cuchulainn gave it to his charioteer. The charioteer took first then his helm, ridged, like a board (?), four-cornered, with much of every colour and every form, over the middle of his shoulders. This was well-measured (?) to him, and it was not an overweight. His hand brought the circlet of red-yellow, as though it were a plate of red-gold, of refined gold smelted over the edge of an anvil, to his brow, as a sign of his charioteering, in distinction to his master.

He took the goads (?) of his horses, and his whip (?) inlaid in his right hand. He took the reins to hold back his horses in his left hand. [Note: Gloss incorporated in text: 'i. e. to direct his horses, in his left hand, for the great power of his charioteering.'] Then he put the iron inlaid breastplates on the horses, so that they were covered from forehead to forefoot with spears and points and lances and hard points, so that every motion in this chariot was spear-near, so that every corner and every point and every end and every front of this chariot was a way of tearing. It is then that he cast a spell of covering over his horses and over his companion, so that he was not visible to any one in the camp, and so that every one in the camp was visible to them. It was proper that he should cast this, because there were the three gifts of charioteering on the charioteer that day, the leap over ----, and the straight ----, and the ----.

Then the hero and the champion and he who made the fold of the Badb [Note:

The Badb (scald-crow) was a war-goddess. This is an expressive term for the piled-up bodies of the slain.] of the men of the earth, Cuchulainn Mac Sualtaim, took his battle-array of battle and contest and strife. This was his battle-array of battle and contest and strife: he put on twenty-seven skin tunics, waxed, like board, equally thick, which used to be under strings and chains and thongs, against his white skin, that he might not lose his mind nor his understanding when his rage should come. He put on his hero's battle-girdle over it outside, of hard-leather, hard, tanned, of the choice of seven ox-hides of a heifer, so that it covered him from the thin part of his sides to the thick part of his arm-pit; it used to be on him to repel spears, and points, and darts, and lances, and arrows. For they were cast from him just as if it was stone or rock or horn that they struck (?). Then he put on his apron, skin like, silken, with its edge of white gold variegated, against the soft lower part of his body. He put on his dark apron of dark leather, well tanned, of the choice of four ox-hides of a heifer, with his battle-girdle of cows' skins (?) about it over his silken skin-like apron. Then the royal hero took his battle-arms of battle and contest and strife. These then were his battle-arms of battle: he took his ivory-hilted, bright-faced weapon, with his eight little swords; he took his five-pointed spear, with his eight little spears [Note: In the margin: 'and his quiver,' probably an interpolation.]; he took his spear of battle, with his eight little darts; he took his javelin with his eight little javelins; his eight shields of feats, with his round shield, dark red, in which a boar that would be shown at a feast would go into the boss (?), with its edge sharp, keen, very sharp, round about it, so that it would cut hairs against the stream for sharpness and keenness and great sharpness; when the warrior did the edge-feat with it, he would cut equally with his shield, and with his spear, and with his sword.

Then he put on his head a ridged-helmet of battle and contest and strife, from which there was uttered the shout of a hundred warriors, with along cry from every corner and every angle of it. For there used to cry from it equally goblins and sprites and ghosts of the glen and demons of the air, before and above and around, wherever he used to go before shedding the blood of warriors and enemies. There was cast over him his dress of concealment by the garment of the Land of Promise that was given by his foster-father in wizardry.

It is then came the first contortion on Cuchulainn, so that it made him horrible, many-shaped, wonderful, strange. His shanks shook like a tree before the stream, or like a rush against the stream, every limb and every joint and every end and every member, of him from head to foot. He made a ---- of rage of his body inside his skin. His feet and his shins and his knees came so that they were behind him; his heels and his calves and his hams came so that they were in front. The front-sinews of his calves came so that they were on the front of his shins, so that every huge knot of them was as great as a warrior's clenched fist. The temple-sinews of his head were stretched, so that they were on the hollow of his neck, so that every round lump of them, very great, innumerable, not to be equalled (?), measureless, was as great as the head of a month old child.

Then he made a red bowl of his face and of his visage on him; he swallowed one of his two eyes into his head, so that from his cheek a wild crane could hardly have reached it [to drag it] from the back of his skull. The other sprang out till it was on his cheek outside. His lips were marvellously contorted. Tie drew the cheek from the jawbone, so that his gullet was visible. His lungs and his lights came so that they were flying in his mouth and in his throat. He struck a blow of the ---- of a lion with his upper palate on the roof of his skull, so that every flake of fire that came into his mouth from his throat was as large as a wether's skin. His heart was heard light-striking (?) against his ribs like the roaring of a bloodhound at its food, or like a lion going through bears. There were seen the palls of the Badb, and the rain-clouds of poison, and the sparks of fire very red in clouds and in vapours over his head with the boiling of fierce rage, that rose over him.

His hair curled round his head like the red branches of a thorn in the gap of Atalta (?). Though a royal apple-tree under royal fruit had been shaken about it, hardly would an apple have reached the ground through it, but an apple would have fixed on every single hair there, for the twisting of the rage that rose from his hair above him.

The hero's light rose from his forehead, so that it was as long, and as thick, as a warrior's whet-stone, so that it was equally long with the nose, till he went mad in playing with the shields, in pressing on (?) the charioteer, in ---- the hosts. As high, as thick, as strong, as powerful, as long, as the mast of a great ship, was the straight stream of dark blood that rose straight up from the very top of his head, so that it made a dark smoke of wizardry like the smoke of a palace when the king comes to equip himself in the evening of a wintry day.

After that contortion wherewith Cuchulainn was contorted, then the hero of valour sprang into his scythed battle-chariot, with its iron points, with its thin edges, with its hooks, and with its hard points, with its sharp points (?) of a hero, with their pricking goads (?), with its nails of sharpness that were on shafts and thongs and cross-pieces and ropes (?) of that chariot.

It was thus the chariot was, with its body thin-framed (?), dry-framed (?), feat-high, straight-shouldered (?), of a champion, on which there would have been room for eight weapons fit for a lord, with the speed of swallow or of wind or of deer across the level of the plain. The chariot was placed on two horses, swift, vehement, furious, small-headed, small-round, small-end, pointed, ----, red-breasted, ----, easy to recognise, well-yoked, ... One of these two horses was supple, swift-leaping, great of strength, great of curve, great of foot, great of length, ----. The other horse was flowing-maned, slender-footed, thin-footed, slender-heeled, ----.

It is then that he threw the thunder-feat of a hundred, and the thunder-feat of four hundred, and he stopped at the thunder-feat of five hundred, for he did not think it too much for this equal number to fall by him in his first attack, and in his first contest of battle on the four provinces of Ireland; and he came forth in this way to attack his enemies, and he took his chariot in a great circuit about the four great provinces of Ireland, and he put the attack of an enemy among enemies on them. And a heavy course was put on his chariot, and the iron wheels of the chariot went into the ground, so that it was enough for fort and fortress, the way the iron wheels of the chariot went into the ground; for there arose alike turfs and stones and rocks and flagstones and gravel of the ground as high as the iron wheels of the chariot.

The reason why he cast the circle of war round about the four great provinces of Ireland, was that they might not flee from him, and that they might not scatter, that he might make sure of them, to avenge the boys on them; and he comes into the battle thus in the middle, and overthrew great fences of his enemies' corpses round about the host thrice, and puts the attack of an enemy among enemies on them, so that they fell sole to sole, and neck to neck; such was the density of the slaughter.

He went round again thrice thus, so that he left a layer of six round them in the great circuit; i.e. soles of three to necks of three in the course of a circuit round the camp. So that its name in the Foray is Sesrech Breslige, and it is one of the three not to be numbered in the Foray; i.e. Sesrech Breslige and Imslige Glendamnach and the battle on Garach and Irgarach, except that it was alike dog and horse and man there.

This is what others say, that Lug Mac Ethlend fought along with Cuchulainn the Sesrech Breslige. Their number is not known, and it is impossible to count what number fell there of the rabble. But the chief only have been counted. These are the names of the princes and chiefs: two Cruads, two Calads, two Cirs, two Ciars, two Ecells, three Croms, three Caurs, three Combirge, four Feochars, four Furachars, four Cass, four Fotas, five Caurs, five Cermans, five Cobthachs, six Saxans, six Dachs, six Dares, seven Rochads, seven Ronans, seven Rurthechs, eight Roclads, eight Rochtads, eight Rindachs, eight Corpres, eight Mulachs, nine Daigs, nine Dares, nine Damachs, ten Fiachs, ten Fiachas, ten Fedelmids.

Ten kings over seven fifties did Cuchulainn slay in Breslech Mor in Mag Murthemne; and an innumerable number besides of dogs and horses and women and boys and people of no consequence and rabble. For there did not escape one man out of three of the men of Ireland without a thigh-bone or half his head or one eye broken, or without being marked for ever. And he came from them after giving them battle without wound or blood-stain on himself or on his servant or on either of his horses.

Cuchulainn came next day to survey the host and to show his soft fair form to the women and the troops of women and the girls and the maidens and the poets and the bards, for he did not hold in honour or dignity that haughty form of wizardry that had appeared to them on him the night before. Therefore he came to show his soft fair form that day.

Fair indeed the boy who came then to show his form to the hosts, that is, Cuchulainn Mac Sualtaim. The appearance of three heads of hair on him, dark against the skin of his head, blood-red in the middle, a crown gold-yellow which covers them. A fair arrangement of this hair so that it makes three circles round the hollow of the back of his head, so that each hair ----, dishevelled, very golden, excellent, in long curls, distinguished, fair-coloured, over his shoulders, was like gold thread.

A hundred ringlets, bright purple, of red-gold, gold-flaming, round his neck; a hundred threads with mixed carbuncle round his head. Four dimples in each of his two cheeks; that is, a yellow dimple, and a green dimple, and a blue dimple, and a purple dimple. Seven gems of brilliance of an eye, in each of his two royal eyes. Seven toes on each of his two feet, seven fingers on each of his two hands, with the grasp of a hawk's claws, with the seizure of a griffin's claws on each of them separately.

Then he puts on his feast-dress that day. This was his raiment on him: a fair tunic, proper; bright-purple, with a border with five folds. A white brooch of white silver with adorned gold inlaid over his white breast, as if it was a lantern full of light, that the eyes of men could not look at for its splendour and its brightness. A silken tunic of silk against his skin so that it covered him to the top of his dark apron of dark-red, soldierly, royal, silken.

A dark shield; dark red, dark purple, with five chains of gold, with a rim of white metal on it. A sword gold-hilted, inlaid with ivory hilt of red-gold raised high on his girdle. A spear, long, grey-edged, with a spear-head sharp, attacking, with rivets of gold, gold-flaming by him in the chariot. Nine heads in one of his two hands, and ten heads in the other hand. He shook them from him towards the hosts. So that this is the contest of a night to Cuchulainn. Then the women of Connaught raised themselves on the hosts, and the women were climbing on the men to look at Cuchulainn's form. Medb hid her face and dare not show her face, but was under the shield-shelter for fear of Cuchulainn. So that it is hence Dubthach Doeltenga of Ulster said:

'If it is the Riastartha, there will be corpses
Of men therefrom,' etc. [Note: Rhetoric, fifty-four lines.]
Fiacha Fialdana from Imraith (?) came to speak with the son of his mother's sister, Mane Andoe his name. Docha Mac Magach went with Mane Andoe: Dubthach Doeltenga of Ulster came with Fiacha Fialdana from Imraith (?). Docha threw a spear at Fiacha, so that it went into Dubthach. Then Dubthach threw a spear at Mane, so that it went into Docha. The mothers of Dubthach and Docha were two sisters. Hence is Imroll Belaig Euin. [Note: i.e. the Random Throw of Belach Euin.]

(Or Imroll Belaig Euin is from this: the hosts go to Belach Euin, their two troops wait there. Diarmait Mac Conchobair comes from the north from Ulster.

'Let a horseman go from you,' said Diarmait, 'that Mane may come to speak with me with one man, and I will come with one man to meet him.' They meet then.

I have come,' said Diarmait, 'from Conchobar, who says to Medb and Ailill, that they let the cows go, and make whole all that they have done there, and bring the Bull [Note: i.e. bring Findbennach to meet the Dun of Cualnge.] from the west hither to the Bull, that they may meet, because Medb has promised it.'

'I will go and tell them,' said Mane. He tells this then to Medb and Ailill.

'This cannot be got of Medb,' said Mane.

'Let us exchange arms then, 'said Diarmait, 'if you think it better.'

'I am content,' said Mane. Each of them throws his spear at the other, so that the two of them die, and so that the name of this place is Imroll Belaig Euin.)

Their forces rush at each other: there fall three twenties of them in each of the forces. Hence is Ard-in-Dirma. [Note: The Height of the Troop.]

Ailill's folk put his king's crown on Tamun the fool; Ailill dare not have it on himself. Cuchulainn threw a stone at him at Ath Tamuin, so that his head broke thereby. Hence is Ath Tamuin and Tuga-im-Tamun. [Note: i.e., Covering about Tamun.]

Then Oengus, son of Oenlam the Fair, a bold warrior of Ulster, turned all the host at Moda Loga (that is the same as Lugmod) as far as Ath Da Ferta: He did not let them go past, and he pelted them with stones, and the learned say ---- before till they should go under the sword at Emain Macha, if it had been in single combat that they had come against him. Fair-play was broken on him, and they slew him in an unequal fight.

'Let some one come from you against me,' said Cuchulainn at Ath Da Ferta.

'It will not be I, it will not be I,' said every one from his place. 'A scapegoat is not owed from my race, and if it were owed, it would not be I whom they would give in his stead for a scapegoat.'

Then Fergus Mac Roich was asked to go against him. He refuses to go against his foster-son Cuchulainn. Wine was given to him, and he was greatly intoxicated, and he was asked about going to the combat. He goes forth then since they were urgently imploring him.

Then Cuchulainn said: 'It is with my security that you come against me, O friend Fergus,' said he, 'with no sword in its place.' For Ailill had stolen it, as we said before.

'I do not care at all,' said Fergus; 'though there were a sword there, it would not be plied on you. Give way to me, O Cuchulainn,' said Fergus.

'You will give way to me in return then,' said Cuchulainn.

'Even so,' said Fergus.

Then Cuchulainn fled back before Fergus as far as Grellach Doluid, that Fergus might give way to him on the day of the battle. Then Cuchulainn sprang in to Grellach Doluid.

'Have you his head, O Fergus?' said every one.

'No,' said Fergus, 'it is not like a tryst. He who is there is too lively for me. Till my turn comes round again, I will not go.'

Then they go past him, and take camp at Crich Ross. Then Ferchu, an exile, who was in exile against Ailill, hears them. He comes to meet Cuchulainn. Thirteen men was his number. Cuchulainn kills Ferchu's warriors. Their thirteen stones are there.

Medb sent Mand of Muresc, son of Daire, of the Domnandach, to fight Cuchulainn. Own brothers were lie and Fer Diad, and two sons of one father. This Mand was a man fierce and excessive in eating and sleeping, a man ill-tongued, foul-mouthed, like Dubthach Doeltenga of Ulster. He was a man strong, active, with strength of limb like Munremar Mac Gerrcind; a fiery warrior like Triscod Trenfer of Conchobar's house.

'I will go, and I unarmed, and I will grind him between my hands, for I deem it no honour or dignity to ply weapons on a beardless wild boy such as he.'

He went then to seek Cuchulainn. He and his charioteer were there on the plain watching the host.

'One man coming towards us,' said Loeg to Cuchulainn.

'What kind of man?' said Cuchulainn.

'A man black, dark, strong, bull-like, and he unarmed.'

'Let him come past you,' said Cuchulainn.

He came to them therewith.

To fight against you have I come,' said Mand.

Then they begin to wrestle for a long time, and Mand overthrows Cuchulainn thrice, so that the charioteer urged him.

'If you had a strife for the hero's portion in Emain,' said he, 'you would be mighty over the warriors of Emain!'

His hero's rage comes, and his warrior's fury rises, so that he overthrew Mand against the pillar, so that he falls in pieces. Hence is Mag Mand Achta, that is, Mand Echta, that is, Mand's death there.

[From the Yellow Book of Lecan]

On the morrow Medb sent twenty-seven men to Cuchulainn's bog. Fuilcarnn is the name of the bog, on this side of Fer Diad's Ford. They threw their twenty-nine spears at him at once; i.e. Gaile-dana with his twenty-seven sons and his sister's son, Glas Mac Delgna. When then they all stretched out their hands to their swords, Fiacha Mac Fir-Febe came after them out of the camp. He gave a leap from his chariot when he saw all their hands against Cuchulainn, and he strikes off the arms of the twenty-nine of them.

Then Cuchulainn said: 'What you have done I deem help at the nick of time (?).'

'This little,' said Fiacha, 'is a breach of compact for us Ulstermen. If any of them reaches the camp, we will go with our cantred under the point of the sword.'

'I swear, etc., since I have emitted my breath,' said Cuchulainn, 'not a man of them shall reach it alive.'

Cuchulainn slew then the twenty-nine men and the two sons of Ficce with them, two bold warriors of Ulster who came to ply their might on the host. This is that deed on the Foray, when they went to the battle with Cuchulainn.

This is the Combat of Fer Diad and Cuchulainn

Then they considered what man among them would be fit to ward off Cuchulainn. The four provinces of Ireland spoke, and confirmed, and discussed, whom it would be fitting to send to the ford against Cuchulainn. All said that it was the Horn-skin from Irrus Domnand, the weight that is not supported, the battle-stone of doom, his own dear and ardent foster-brother. For Cuchulainn had not a feat that he did not possess, except it were the Gae Bolga alone; and they thought he could avoid it, and defend himself against it, because of the horn about him, so that neither arms nor many edges pierced it.

Medb sent messengers to bring Fer Diad. Fer Diad did not come with those messengers. Medb sent poets and bards and satirists [Note: Ir. **aes glantha gemaidi**, the folk who brought blotches on the cheeks (i.e. by their lampoons).] to him, that they might satirise him and mock him and put him to ridicule, that he might not find a place for his head in the world, until he should come to the tent of Medb and Ailill on the Foray. Fer Diad came with those messengers, for the fear of their bringing shame on him.

Findabair, the daughter of Medb and Ailill, was put on one side of him: it is Findabair who put her hand on every goblet and on every cup of Fer Diad; it is she who gave him three kisses at every cup of them; it is she who distributed apples right frequent over the bosom of his tunic. This is what she said: that he, Fer Diad, was her darling and her chosen wooer of the men of the world.

When Fer Diad was satisfied and happy and very joyful, Medb said:

'Ale! O Fer Diad, do you know why you have been summoned into this tent?'

'I do not know indeed,' said Fer Diad; 'except that the nobles of the men of Ireland are there. What is there less fitting for me to be there than for any other good warrior?'

'It is not that indeed,' said Medb; 'but to give you a chariot worth three sevens of cumals [See previous note about *cumal*.] and the equipment of twelve men, and the equal of Mag Murthemne from the arable land of Mag Ai; and that you should be in Cruachan always, and wine to be poured for you there; and freedom of your descendants and of your race for ever without tribute or tax; my leaf-shaped brooch of gold to be given to you, in which there are ten score ounces and ten score half-ounces, and ten score *crosach* and ten score quarters; Findabair, my daughter and Ailill's daughter, for your one wife, and you shall get my love if you need it over and above.'

'He does not need it,' said every, one: 'great are the rewards and gifts.'

'That is true,' said Fer Diad, 'they are great; and though they are great, O Medb, it is with you yourself they will be left, rather than that I should go against my foster-brother to battle.'

'O men,' said she, said Medb (through the right way of division and setting by the ears), 'true is the word that Cuchulainn spoke,' as if she had not heard Fer Diad at all.

'What word is this, O Medb?' said Fer Diad.

'He said indeed,' said she, 'that he would not think it too much that you should fall by him as the first fruits of his prowess in the province to which he should come.'

'To say that was not fitting for him. For it is not weariness or cowardice that he has ever known in me, day nor night. I swear, etc., [Note: The usual oath, 'by the god by whom my people swear,' understood.] that I will be the first man who will come to-morrow morning to the ford of combat.'

'May victory and blessing come to you,' said Medb. 'And I think it better that weariness or cowardice be found with you, because of friendship beyond my own men (?). Why is it more fitting for him to seek the good of Ulster because his mother was of them, than for you to seek the good of the province of Connaught, because you are the son of a king of Connaught?'

It is thus they were binding their covenants and their compact, and they made a song there:

'Thou shalt have a reward,' etc.

There was a wonderful warrior of Ulster who witnessed that bargaining, and that was Fergus Mac Roich. Fergus came to his tent.

'Woe is me! the deed that is done to-morrow morning!' said Fergus.

'What deed is that?' said the folk in the tent.

'My good fosterling Cuchulainn to be slain.'

'Good lack! who makes that boast?'

'An easy question: his own dear ardent foster-brother, Fer Diad Mac Damain. Why do ye not win my blessing?' said Fergus; 'and let one of you go with a warning and with compassion to Cuchulainn, if perchance he would leave the ford to-morrow morning.'

'On our conscience,' said they, 'though it were you yourself who were on the ford of combat, we would not come as far as [the ford] to seek you.'

'Good, my lad,' said Fergus; 'get our horses for us and yoke the chariot.'

The lad arose and got the horses and yoked the chariot. They came forth to the ford of combat where Cuchulainn was.

'One chariot coming hither towards us, O Cuchulainn!' said Loeg. For it is thus the lad was, with his back towards his lord. He used to win every other game of **brandub** [*Brandub*, the name of a game; probably, like **fidchill** and **buanfach**, of the nature of chess or draughts.] and of chess-playing from his master: the sentinel and watchman on the four quarters of Ireland over and above that.

'What kind of chariot then?' said Cuchulainn.

'A chariot like a huge royal fort, with its yolcs strong golden, with its great panel(?) of copper, with its shafts of bronze, with its body thin-framed (?), dry-framed (?), feat-high, scythed, sword-fair (?), of a champion, on two horses, swift, stout(?), well-yoked (?), ---- (?). One royal warrior, wide-eyed, was the combatant of the chariot. A beard curly, forked, on him, so that it reached over the soft lower part of his soft shirt, so that it would shelter (?) fifty warriors to be under the heavy ---- of the warrior's beard, on a day of storm and rain. A round shield, white, variegated, many-coloured on him, with three chains ----, so that there would be room from front to back for four troops of ten men behind the leather of the shield which is upon the ---- of the warrior. A sword, long, hard-edged, red-broad in the sheath, woven and twisted of white silver, over the skin of the bold-in-battle. A spear, strong, three-ridged, with a winding and with bands of white silver all white by him across the chariot.'

'Not hard the recognition,' said Cuchulainn; 'my friend Fergus comes there, with a warning and with compassion to me before all the four provinces.'

Fergus reached them and sprang from his chariot and Cuchulainn greeted him.

'Welcome your coming, O my friend, O Fergus,' said Cuchulainn.

'I believe your welcome,' said Fergus.

'You may believe it,' said Cuchulainn; 'if a flock of birds come to the plain, you shall have a duck with half of another; if fish come to the estuaries, you shall have a salmon with half of another; a sprig of watercress, and a sprig of marshwort, and a sprig of seaweed, and a drink of cold sandy water after it.'

'That portion is that of an outlaw,' said Fergus.

'That is true, it is an outlaw's portion that I have,' said Cuchulainn, 'for I have been from the Monday after Samain to this time, and I have not gone for a night's entertainment, through strongly obstructing the men of Ireland on the Cattle-Foray of Cualnge at this time.'

'If it were for this we came,' said Fergus, 'we should have thought it the better to leave it; and it is not for this that we have come.'

'Why else have you come to me?' said Cuchulainn.

'To tell you the warrior who comes against you in battle and combat to-morrow morning,' said he.

'Let us find it out and let us hear it from you then,' said Cuchulainn.

'Your own foster-brother, Fer Diad Mac Damain.'

'On our word, we think it not best that it should be he we come to meet,'said Cuchulainn, 'and it is not for fear of him but for the greatness of our love for him.'

'It is fitting to fear him,' said Fergus, 'for he has a skin of horn in battle against a man, so that neither weapon nor edge will pierce it.'

'Do not say that at all,' said Cuchulainn, 'for I swear the oath that my people swear, that every joint and every limb of him will be as pliant as a pliant rush in the midst of a stream under the point of my sword, if he shows himself once to me on the ford.'

It is thus they were speaking, and they made a song:

'O Cuchulainn, a bright meeting,' etc.

After that, 'Why have you come, O my friend, O Fergus?' said Cuchulainn.

'That is my purpose,' said Fergus.

'Good luck and profit,' said Cuchulainn, 'that no other of the men of Ireland has come for this purpose, unless the four provinces of Ireland all met at one time. I think nothing of a warning before a single warrior.'

Then Fergus went to his tent.

As regards the charioteer and Cuchulainn:

'What shall you do to-night?' said Loeg.

'What indeed?' said Cuchulainn.

'It is thus that Fer Diad will come to seek you, with new beauty of plaiting and haircutting, and washing and bathing, and the four provinces of Ireland with him to look at the fight. It would please me if you went to the place where you will get the same adorning for yourself, to the place where is Emer of the Beautiful Hair, to Cairthend of Cluan Da Dam in Sliab Fuait.'

So Cuchulainn went thither that night, and spent the night with his own wife. His adventures from this time are not discussed here now. As to Fer Diad, he came to his tent; it was gloomy and weary that Fer Diad's tent-servants were that night. They thought it certain that where the two pillars of the battle of the world should meet, that both would fall; or the issue of it would be, that it would be their own lord who would fall there. For it was not easy to fight with Cuchulainn on the Foray.

There were great cares on Fer Diad's mind that night, so that they did not let him sleep. One of his great anxieties was that he should let pass from him all the treasures that had been offered to him, and the maiden, by reason of combat with one man. If he did not fight with that one man, he must fight with the six warriors on the morrow. His care that was greater than this was that if he should show himself once on the ford to Cuchulainn, he was certain that he himself would not have power of his head or life thereafter; and Fer Diad arose early on the morrow.

'Good, my lad,' said he, 'get our horses for us, and harness the chariot.'

'On our word,' said the servant, 'we think it not greater praise to go this journey than not to go it.'

He was talking with his charioteer, and he made this little song, inciting his charioteer:

'Let us go to this meeting,' etc.

The servant got the horses and yoked the chariot, and they went forth from the camp.

'My lad,' said Fer Diad, 'it is not fitting that we make our journey without farewell to the men of Ireland. Turn the horses and the chariot for us towards the men of Ireland.'

The servant turned the horses and the chariot thrice towards the men of Ireland. ...

'Does Ailill sleep now?' said Medb.

'Not at all,' said Ailill.

'Do you hear your new son-in-law greeting you?'

'Is that what he is doing?' said Ailill.

'It is indeed,' said Medb, 'and I swear by what my people swear, the man who makes the greeting yonder will not come back to you on the same feet.'

'Nevertheless we have profited by(?) the good marriage connection with him,' said Ailill; 'provided Cuchulainn fell by him, I should not care though they both fell. But we should think it better for Fer Diad to escape.'

Fer Diad came to the ford of combat.

'Look, my lad,' said Fer Diad; 'is Cuchulainn on the ford?'

'He is not, indeed,' said the servant.

'Look well for us,' said Fer Diad.

'Cuchulainn is not a little speck in hiding where he would be,' said the lad.

'It is true, O boy, until to-day Cuchulainn has not heard of the coming of a good warrior [Note: Gloss incorporated in the text: 'or a good man.'] against him on the Cattle Foray of Cualnge, and when he has heard of it he has left the ford.'

'A great pity to slander Cuchulainn in his absence! For do you remember how when you gave battle to German Garbglas above the edge-borders of the Tyrrhene Sea, you left your sword with the hosts, and it was Cuchulainn who killed a hundred warriors in reaching it, and he brought it to you; and do you remember where we were that night?' said the lad.

'I do not know it,' said Fer Diad.

'At the house of Scathach's steward,' said the lad, 'and you went ---- and haughtily before us into the house first. The churl gave you a blow with the three-pointed flesh-hook in the small of your back, so that it threw you out over the door like a shot. Cuchulainn came into the house and gave the churl a blow with his sword, so that it made two pieces of him. It was I who was steward for you while you were in that place. If only for that day, you should not say that you are a better warrior than Cuchulainn.'

'What you have done is wrong,' said Fer Diad, 'for I would not have come to seek the combat if you had said it to me at first. Why do you not pull the cushions [Note: LL *fortchai*. YBL has *feirtsi*, 'shafts.'] of the chariot under my side and my skin-cover under my head, so that I might sleep now?'

'Alas!' said the lad, 'it is the sleep of a fey man before deer and hounds here.'

'What, O lad, are you not fit to keep watch and ward for me?'

'I am fit,' said the lad; 'unless men come in clouds or in mist to seek you, they will not come at all from east or west to seek you without warning and observation.'

The cushions [Note: LL *fortchai*. YBL has *feirtsi*, 'shafts.'] of his chariot were pulled under his side and the skin under his head. And yet he could not sleep a little.

As to Cuchulainn it is set forth:

'Good, O my friend, O Loeg, take the horses and yoke the chariot; if Fer Diad is waiting for us, he is thinking it long.'

The boy rose and took the horses and yoked the chariot.

Cuchulainn stepped into his chariot and they came on to the ford. As to Fer Diad's servant, he had not long to watch till he heard the creaking of the chariot coming towards them. He took to waking his master, and made a song:

'I hear a chariot,' etc.

(This is the description of Cuchulainn's chariot: one of the three chief chariots of the narration on the Cattle Foray of Cualnge.)

'How do you see Cuchulainn?' said he, said Fer Diad, to his charioteer.

'I see,' said he, 'the chariot broad above, fine, of white crystal, with a yoke of gold with ---- (?), with great panels of copper, with shafts of bronze, with tyres of white metal, with its body thin-framed (?) dry-framed (?), feat-high, sword-fair (?), of a champion, on which there would be room for seven arms fit for a lord (?). A fair seat for its lord; so that this chariot, Cuchulainn's chariot, would reach with the speed of a swallow or of a wild deer, over the level land of Mag Slebe. That is the speed and ---- which they attain, for it is towards us they go. This chariot is at hand on two horses small-headed, small-round, small-end, pointed, ----, red-breasted, ----, easy to recognise, well-yoked. ... One of the two horses is supple(?), swift-leaping, great of strength, great of foot, great of length, ----. The other horse is curly-maned, slender-footed, narrow-footed, heeled, ----. Two wheels dark, black. A pole of metal adorned with red enamel, of a fair colour. Two bridles golden, in-laid. There is a man with fair curly hair, broad cut (?), in the front of this chariot. There is round him a blue mantle, red-purple. A spear with wings (?), and it red, furious; in his clenched fist, red-flaming. The appearance of three heads of hair on him, i.e. dark hair against the skin of his head, hair blood-red in the middle, a crown of gold covers the third hair.

'A fair arrangement of the hair so that it makes three circles round about his shoulders down behind. I think it like gold thread, after its colour has been made over the edge of the anvil; or like the yellow of bees on which the sun shines in a summer day, is the shining of each single hair of his hair. Seven toes on each of his feet, and seven fingers on each of his hands, and the shining of a very great fire round his eye, ---- (?) and the hoofs of his horses; a hero's ---- in his hands.

'The charioteer of the chariot is worthy of him in his presence: curly hair very black has he, broad-cut along his head. A cowl-dress is on him open; two very fine golden leaf-shaped switches in his hand, and a light grey mantle round him, and a goad of white silver in his hand, plying the goad on the horses, whichever way the champion of great deeds goes who was at hand in the chariot.

'He is veteran of his land (?): he and his servant think little of Ireland.'

'Go, O fellow,' said he, said Fer Diad; 'you praise too much altogether; and prepare the arms in the ford against his coming.'

'If I turned my face backwards, it seems to me the chariot would come through the back of my neck.'

'O fellow,' said he, 'too greatly do you praise Cuchulainn, for it is not a reward for praising he has given you'; and it is thus he was giving his description, and he said:

'The help is timely,' etc.

It is not long afterwards that they met in the middle of the ford, and Fer Diad said to Cuchulainn:

'Whence come you, O Cua?' said he (for [Note: An interpolation.] *cua* was the name of squinting in old Gaelic; and there were seven pupils in Cuchulainn's royal eye, and two of these pupils were squinting, and the ugliness of it is no greater than its beauty on him; and if there had been a greater blemish on Cuchulainn, it is that with which he reproached him; and he was proclaiming it); and he made a song, and Cuchulainn answered:

'Whence art thou come, O Hound,' etc.

Then Cuchulainn said to his charioteer that he was to taunt him when he was overcome, and that he was to praise him when he was victorious, in the combat against Fer Diad. Then the charioteer said to him:

'The man goes over thee as the tail over a cat; he washes thee as foam is washed in water, he squeezes (?) thee as a loving mother her son.'

Then they took to the ford-play. Scathach's ---- (?)came to them both. Fer Diad and Cuchulainn performed marvellous feats. Cuchulainn went and leapt into Fer Diad's shield; Fer Diad hurled him from him thrice into the ford; so that the charioteer taunted him again ---- and he swelled like breath in a bag.

His size increased till he was greater than Fer Diad.

'Give heed to the ***Gae bolga***,' said the charioteer; he sent it to him along the stream.

Cuchulainn seized it between his toes, and wielded it on Fer Diad, into his body's armour. It advances like one spear, so that it became twenty-four points. Then Fer Diad turned the shield below. Cuchulainn thrust at him with the spear over the shield, so that it broke the shaft of his ribs and went through Fer Diad's heart.

[***Fer Diad***:] 'Strong is the ash from thy right hand! The ---- rib breaks, my heart is blood. Well hast thou given battle! I fall, O Hound.'

[***Cuchulainn***:] 'Alas, O golden brooch, O Fer Diad! ----, O fair strong striker! Thy hand was victorious; our dear foster brotherhood, O delight of the eyes! Thy shield with the rim of gold, thy sword was dear. Thy ring of white silver round thy noble arm. Thy chess-playing was worthy of a great man. Thy cheek fair-purple; thy yellow curling hair was great, it was a fair treasure. Thy soft folded girdle which used to be about thy side. That thou shouldst fall at Cuchulainn's hands was sad, O Calf! Thy shield did not suffice which used to be for service. Our combat with thee is not fitting, our horses and our tumult. Fair was the great hero! every host used to be defeated and put under foot. Alas, O golden brooch, O Fer Diad!'

THIS IS THE LONG WARNING OF SUALTAIM

While the things that we have related were done, Suallaith heard from Rath Sualtaim in Mag Murthemne the vexing of his son Cuchulainn against twelve sons of Gaile Dana [Note: LL, 'Twenty-seven sons of Calatin.' In the story as related earlier in YBL it is 'Gaile Dana with his twenty-seven sons.'] and his sister's son. It is then that Sualtaim said:

'Is it heaven that bursts, or the sea over its boundaries, or earth that is destroyed, or the shout of my son against odds?'

Then he comes to his son. Cuchulainn was displeased that he should come to him.

'Though he were slain, I should not have strength to avenge him. Go to the Ulstermen,' says Cuchulainn, 'and let them give battle to the warriors at once; if they do not give it, they will not be avenged for ever.'

When his father saw him, there was not in his chariot as much as the point of a rush would cover that was not pierced. His left hand which the shield protected, twenty wounds were in it.

Sualtaim came over to Emain and shouted to the Ulstermen:

'Men are being slain, women carried off, cows driven away!'

His first shout was from the side of the court; his second from the side of the fortress; the third shout was on the mound of the hostages in Emain. No one answered; it was the practice of the Ulstermen that none of them should speak except to Conchobar; and Conchobar did not speak before the three druids.

'Who takes them, who steals them, who carries them off?' said the druid.

Ailill Mac Mata carries them off and steals them and takes them, through the guidance of Fergus Mac Roich,' said Sualtaim. 'Your people have been enslaved as far as Dun Sobairce; their cows and their women and their cattle have been taken. Cuchulainn did not let them into Mag Murthemne and into Crich Rois; three months of winter then, bent branches of hazel held together his dress upon him. Dry wisps are on his wounds. He has been wounded so that he has been parted joint from joint.'

'Fitting,' said the druid, 'were the death of the man who has spurred on the king.'

'It is fitting for him,' said Conchobar.

'It is fitting for him,' said the Ulstermen.

'True is what Sualtaim says,' said Conchobar; 'from the Monday night of Samain to the Monday night of Candlemas he has been in this foray.'

Sualtaim gave a leap out thereupon. He did not think sufficient the answer that he had. He falls on his shield, so that the engraved edge of the shield cut his head off. His head is brought back into Emain into the house on the shield, and the head says the same word (though some say that he was asleep on the stone, and that he fell thence on to his shield in awaking).

'Too great was this shout,' said Conchobar. 'The sea before them, the heaven over their tops, the earth under their feet. I will bring every cow into its milking-yard, and every woman and every boy from their house, after the victory in battle.'

Then Conchobar struck his hand on his son, Findchad Fer m-Bend. Hence he is so called because there were horns of silver on him.

THE MUSTER OF THE ULSTERMEN

'Arise, O Findchad, I will send thee to Deda,' etc. [Note: Rhetoric, followed by a long list of names.]

It was not, difficult for Findchad to take his message, for they were, the whole province of Conchobar, every chief of them, awaiting Conchobar; every one was then east and north and west of Emain. When they were there, they all came till they were at Emain Macha. When they were there, they Beard the uprising of Conchobar in Emain. They went past Emain southwards after the host. Their first march then was from Emain to Irard Cuillend.

'What are you waiting for here?' said Conchobar.

'Waiting for your sons,' said the host. 'They have gone with thirty with them to Temair to seek Eirc, son of Coirpre Niafer and Fedelm Noicride. Till their two cantreds should come to us, we will not go from this place.'

'I will not remain indeed,' said Conchobar, 'till the men of Ireland know that I have awaked from the sickness in which I was.'

Conchobar and Celtchar went with three fifties of chariots, and they brought eight twenties of heads from Ath Airthir Midi; hence is Ath Fene. They were there watching the host. And eight twenties of women, that was their share of the spoil. Their heads were brought there, and Conchobar and Celtchar sent them to the camp. It is there that Celtchar said to Conchobar: [Note: Rhetoric.]

(Or it was Cuscraid, the Stammerer of Macha, son of Conchobar, sang this song the night before the battle, after the song which Loegaire Buadach had sung, to wit, 'Arise, kings of Macha,' etc., and it would be in the camp it was sung.)

It was in this night that the vision happened to Dubthach Doeltenga of Ulster, when the hosts were on Garach and Irgarach. It is there that he said in his sleep:

THE VISION OF DUBTHACH

'A wonder of a morning,' [Note: Rhetoric.] a wonder of a time, when hosts will be confused, kings will be turned, necks will break, the sun will grow red, three hosts will be routed by the track of a host about Conchobar. They will strive for their women, they will chase their flocks in fight on the morning, heroes will be smitten, dogs will be checked (?), horses will be pressed (?), ---- ----, ---- will drip, from the assemblies of great peoples.'

Therewith they awoke through their sleep (?). The Nemain threw the host into confusion there; a hundred men of them died. There is silence there then; when they heard Cormac Condlongas again (or it is Ailill Mac Matae in the camp who sang this):

'The time of Ailill. Great his truce, the truce of Cuillend,' etc. [Note: Rhetoric.]

THE MARCH OF THE COMPANIES

While these things were being done, the Connaughtman determined to send messengers by the counsel of Ailill and Medb and Fergus, to look at the Ulstermen, to see whether they had reached the plain. It is there that Ailill said:

'Go, O Mac Roth,' said Ailill, 'and look for us whether the men are all(?) in the plain of Meath in which we are. If they have not come, I have carried off their spoil and their cows; let them give battle to me, if it suits them. I will not await them here any longer.'

Then Mac Roth went to look at and to watch the plain. He came back to Ailill and Medb and Fergus The first time then that Mac Roth looked from the circuit of Sliab Fuait, he saw that all the wild beast came out of the wood, so that they were all in the plain.

'The second time,' said Mac Roth, 'that I surveyed the plain, I saw a heavy mist that filled the glens and the valleys, so that it made the hills between them like islands in lakes. Then there appeared to me sparks of fire out of this great mist: there appeared to me a variegation of every different colour in the world. I saw then lightning and din and thunder and a great wind that almost took my hair from my head, and threw me on my back; and yet the wind of the day was not great.'

'What is it yonder, O Fergus?' said Ailill. 'Say what it means.' [Note: Literally, 'is like.']

'That is not hard; this is what it means,' said Fergus: 'This is the Ulstermen after coming out of their sickness. It is they who have come into the wood. The throng and the greatness and the violence of the heroes, it is that which has shaken the wood; it is before them that the wild beasts have fled into the plain. The heavy mist that you saw, which filled the valleys, was the breath of those warriors, which filled the glens so that it made the hills between them like islands in lakes. The lightning and the sparks of fire and the many colours that you saw, O Mac Roth,' said Fergus, 'are the eyes of the warriors from their heads which have shone to you like sparks of fire. The thunder and the din and the noise(?) that you heard, was the whistling of the swords and of the ivory-hilted weapons, the clatter of arms, the creaking of the chariots, the beating of the hoofs of the horses, the strength of the warriors, the roar of the fighting-men, the noise of the soldiers, the great rage and anger and fierceness of the heroes going in madness to the battle, for the greatness of the rage and of the fury(?). They would think they would not reach it at all,' said Fergus.

'We will await them,' said Ailill; 'we have warriors for them.'

'You will need that,' said Fergus, 'for there will not be found in all Ireland, nor in the west of the world, from Greece and Scythia westward to the Orkneys and to the Pillars of Hercules and to the Tower of Bregon and to the island of Gades, any one who shall endure the Ulstermen in their fury and in their rage,' said Fergus.

Then Mac Roth went again to look at the march of the men of Ulster, so that he was in their camp at Slemon Midi, and Fergus; and he told them certain tidings, and Mac Roth said in describing them:

'A great company has come, of great fury, mighty, fierce, to the hill at Slemon Midi,' said Mac Roth. 'I think there is a cantred therein; they took off their clothing at once, and dug a mound of sods under their leader's seat. A warrior fair and tall and long and high, beautiful, the fairest of kings his form, in the front of the company. Hair white-yellow has he, and it curly, neat, bushy (?), ridged, reaching to the hollow of his shoulders. A tunic curly, purple, folded round him; a brooch excellent, of red-gold, in his cloak on his breast; eyes very grey, very fair, in his head; a face proper, purple, has he, and it narrow below and broad above: a beard forked, very curly, gold-yellow he has; a shirt white, hooded, with red ornamentation, round about him; a sword gold-hilted on his shoulders; a white shield with rivets(?) of gold; abroad grey spear-head on a slender shaft in his hand. The fairest of the princes of the world his march, both in host and rage and form and dress, both in face and terror and battle and triumph, both in prowess and horror and dignity.

'Another company has come there,' said Mac Roth; 'it is next to the other in number and quarrelling and dress and terror and horror. A fair warrior, heroic, is in the front of this company. A green cloak folded round him; a brooch of gold over his arm; hair curly and yellow: an ivory-hilted sword with a hilt of ivory at his left. A shirt with ---- to his knee; a wound-giving shield with engraved edge; the candle of a palace [Note: i.e. spear.] in his hand; a ring of silver about it, and it runs round along the shaft forward to the point, and again it runs to the grip. And that troop sat down on the left hand of the leader of the first troop, and it is thus they sat down, with their knees to the ground, and the rims of their shields against their chins. And I thought there was stammering in the speech of the great fierce warrior who is the leader of that company.

'Another company has come there,' said Mac Roth; 'its appearance is vaster than a cantred; a man brave, difficult, fair, with broad head, before it. Hair dark and curly on him; a beard long, with slender points, forked, has he; a cloak dark-grey, ----, folded round him; a leaf-shaped brooch of white metal over his breast; a white, hooded shirt to his knees; a hero's shield with rivets on him; a sword of white silver about his waist; a five-pointed spear in his hand. He sat down in front of the leader of the first troop.'

'Who is that, O Fergus?' said Ailill.

'I know indeed,' said Fergus, 'those companies. Conchobar, king of a province of Ireland, it is he who has sat down on the mound of sods. Sencha Mac Aililla, the orator of Ulster, it is he who has sat down before him. Cuscraid, the Stammerer of Macha, son of Conchobar, it is he who has sat down at his father's side. It is the custom for the spear that is in his hand in sport yonder before victory ---- before or after. That is a goodly folk for wounding, for essaying every conflict, that has come,' said Fergus.

'They will find men to speak with them here,' said Medb.

'I swear by the god by whom my people swear,' said Fergus, 'there has not been born in Ireland hitherto a man who would check the host of Ulster.' [Note: Conjectural; the line is corrupt in the MS.]

'Another company has come there,' said Mac Roth. 'Greater than a cantred its number. A great warrior, brave, with horror and terror, and he mighty, fiery-faced, before it. Hair dark, greyish on him, and it smooth-thin on his forehead. Around shield with engraved edge on him, a spear five-pointed in his hand, a forked javelin beside him; a hard sword on the back of his head; a purple cloak folded round him; a brooch of gold on his arm; a shirt, white, hooded, to his knee.'

'Who is that, O Fergus?' said Ailill.

'He is the putting of a hand on strife; he is a battle champion for fight; he is judgment against enemies who has come there; that is, Eogan Mac Durthacht, King of Fermoy is that,' said Fergus.

'Another company has come, great, fierce, to the hill at Slemon Midi,' said Mac Roth. 'They have put their clothing behind them. Truly, it is strong, dark, they have come to the hill; heavy is the terror and great the horror which they have put upon themselves; terrible the clash of arms that they made in marching. A man thick of head, brave, like a champion, before it; and he horrible, hideous; hair light, grey on him; eyes yellow, great, in his head; a cloak yellow, with white ---- round about him. A shield, wound-giving, with engraved edge, on him, without; a broad spear, a javelin with a drop of blood along the shaft; and a spear its match with the blood of enemies along its edge in his hand; a great wound-giving sword on his shoulders.'

'Who is that, O Fergus?' said Ailill.

'The man who has so come does not avoid battle or combat or strife: that is, Loegaire the Victorious, Mac Connaid Meic Ilech, from Immail from the north,' said Fergus.

'Another great company has come to Slemon Midi to the hill,' said Mac Roth. 'A warrior thick-necked, fleshy, fair, before that company. Hair black and curly on him, and he purple, blue-faced; eyes grey, shining, in his head; a cloak grey, lordly (?), about him; a brooch of white silver therein; a black shield with a boss of bronze on it; a spear, covered with eyes, with ---- (?), in his hand; a shirt, braided(?), with red ornamentation, about him; a sword with a hilt of ivory over his dress outside.'

'Who is that, O Fergus?' said Ailill.

'He is the putting of a hand on a skirmish; he is the wave of a great sea that drowns little streams; he is a man of three shouts; he is the judgment of ---- of enemies, who so comes,' said Fergus; 'that is, Munremar Mac Gerrcind, from Moduirn in the north.'

'Another great company has come there to the hill to Slemon Midi,' said Mac Roth. 'A company very fair, very beautiful, both in number and strife and raiment. It is fiercely that they make for the hill; the clatter of arms which they raised in going on their course shook the host. A warrior fair, excellent, before the company. Most beautiful of men his form, both in hair and eyes and fear, both in raiment and form and voice and whiteness, both in dignity and size and beauty, both in weapons and knowledge and adornment, both in equipment and armour and fitness, both in honour and wisdom and race.'

'This is his description,' said Fergus; 'he is the brightness of fire, the fair man,

Fedlimid, who so comes there; he is fierceness of warriors, he is the wave of a storm that drowns, he is might that is not endured, with triumphs out of other territories after destruction (?) of his foes; that is Fedlimid ---- ---- there.'

'Another company has come there to the hill to Slemon Midi,' said Mac Roth, 'which is not fewer than a warlike cantred (?). A warrior great, brave, grey, proper, ----, in front of it. Hair black, curly, on him; round eyes, grey(?), very high, in his head. A man bull-like, strong, rough; a grey cloak about him, with a brooch of silver on his arm; a shirt white, hooded, round him; a sword at his side; a red shield with a hard boss of silver on it. A spear with three rivets, broad, in his hand.'

'Who is that, O Fergus?' said Ailill.

'He is the fierce glow of wrath, he is a shaft (?) of every battle; he is the victory of every combat, who has so come there, Connad Mac Mornai from Callann,' said Fergus.

'Another company has come to the hill at Slemon Midi,' said Mac Roth. 'It is the march of an army for greatness. The leader who is in front of that company, not common is a warrior fairer both in form and attire and equipment. Hair bushy, red-yellow, on him; a face proper, purple, well-proportioned; a face narrow below, broad above; lips red, thin; teeth shining, pearly; a voice clear, ringing; a face fair, purple, shapely; most beautiful of the forms of men; a purple cloak folded round him; a brooch with full adornment of gold, over his white breast; a bent shield with many-coloured rivets, with a boss of silver, at his left; a long spear, grey-edged, with a sharp javelin for attack in his hand; a sword gold-hilted, of gold, on his back; a hooded shirt with red ornamentation about him.'

'Who is that, O Fergus?' said Ailill.

'We know, indeed,' said Fergus. 'He is half of a combat truly,' said he, 'who so comes there; he is a fence(?) of battle, he is fierce rage of a bloodhound; Rochad Mac Fathemain from Bridamae, your son-in-law, is that, who wedded your daughter yonder, that is, Findabair.'

'Another company has come to the hill, to Slemon Midi,' said Mac Roth. 'A warrior with great calves, stout, with great thighs, big, in front of that company. Each of his limbs is almost as thick as a man. Truly, he is a man down to the ground,' said he. 'Hair black on him; a face full of wounds, purple, has he; an eye parti-coloured, very high, in his head; a man glorious, dexterous, thus, with horror and terror, who has a wonderful apparel, both raiment and weapons and appearance and splendour and dress; he raises himself with the prowess of a warrior, with achievements of ----, with the pride of wilfulness, with a going through battle to rout overwhelming numbers, with wrath upon foes, with a marching on many hostile countries without protection. In truth, mightily have they come on their course into Slemon Midi.'

'He was ---- of valour and of prowess, in sooth,' said Fergus; 'he was of ---- pride(?) and of haughtiness, he was ---- of strength and dignity, ---- then of armies and hosts of my own foster-brother, Fergus Mac Leiti, King of Line, point of battle of the north of Ireland.'

'Another company, great, fierce, has come to the hill, to Slemon Midi,' said Mac Roth. 'Strife before it, strange dresses on them. A warrior fair, beautiful, before it; gift of every form, both hair and eye and whiteness, both size and strife and fitness; five chains of gold on him; a green cloak folded about him; a brooch of gold in the cloak over his arm; a shirt white, hooded, about him; the tower of a palace in his hand; a sword gold-hilted on his shoulders.'

'Fiery is the bearing of the champion of combat who has so come there,' said Fergus. 'Amorgene, son of Eccet Salach the smith, from Buais in the north is that.'

'Another company has come there, to the hill, to Slemon Midi,' said Mac Roth. It is a drowning for size, it is a fire for splendour, it is a pin for sharpness, it is a battalion for number, it is a rock for greatness, it is ---- for might, it is a judgment for its ----, it is thunder for pride. A warrior rough-visaged, terrible, in front of this company, and he great-bellied, large-lipped; rough hair, a grey beard on him; and he great-nosed, red-limbed; a dark cloak about him, an iron spike on his cloak; a round shield with an engraved edge on him; a rough shirt, braided(?), about him; a great grey spear in his hand, and thirty rivets therein; a sword of seven charges of metal on his shoulders. All the host rose before him, and he overthrew multitudes of the battalion about him in going to the hill.'

'He is a head of strife who has so come,' said Fergus; 'he is a half of battle, he is a warrior for valour, he is a wave of a storm which drowns, he is a sea over boundaries; that is, Celtchar Mac Uithechair from Dunlethglaisi in the north.'

'Another company has come there to the hill, to Slemon Midi,' said Mac Roth. 'A warrior of one whiteness in front of it, all white, both hair and eyelashes and beard and equipment; a shield with a boss of gold on him, and a sword with a hilt of ivory, and a broad spear with rings in his hand. Very heroic has his march come.'

'Dear is the bear, strong-striking, who has so come,' said Fergus; 'the bear of great deeds against enemies, who breaks men, Feradach Find Fechtnach from the grove of Sliab Fuait in the north is that.'

'Another company has come there to the hill, to Slemon Midi,' said Mac Roth. 'A hideous warrior in front of it, and he great-bellied, large-lipped; his lips as big as the lips of a horse; hair dark, curly, on him, and he himself ----, broad-headed, long-handed; a cloak black, hairy, about him; a chain of copper over it, a dark grey buckler over his left hand; a spear with chains in his right hand; a long sword on his shoulders.'

'He is a lion red-handed, fierce of ----, who so comes,' said Fergus. 'He is high of deeds, great in battle, rough; he is a raging on the land who is unendurable, Eirrgi Horse-lipped from Bri Eirge in the north,' said Fergus.

'Another company has come there to the hill, to Slemon Midi,' said Mac Roth. 'Two warriors, fair, both alike, in front of it; yellow hair on them; two white shields with rivets of silver; they are of equal age. They lift up their feet and set them down together; it is not their manner for either of them to lift up his feet without the other. Two heroes, two splendid flames, two points of battle, two warriors, two pillars of fight, two dragons, two fires, two battle-soldiers, two champions of combat, two rods (?), two bold ones, two pets of Ulster about the king.'

'Who are those, O Fergus?' said Ailill.

'Fiachna and Fiacha, two sons of Conchobar Mac Nessa, two darlings of the north of Ireland,' said Fergus.

'Another company has come to the hill, to Slemon Midi,' said Mac Roth. 'Three warriors, fiery, noble, blue-faced, before it. Three heads of hair very yellow have they; three cloaks of one colour in folds about them; three brooches of gold over their arms, three shirts ---- with red ornamentation round about them; three shields alike have they; three swords gold-hilted on their shoulders; three spears, broadgrey, in their right hands. They are of equal age.'

'Three glorious champions of Coba, three of great deeds of Midluachair, three princes of Roth, three veterans of the east of Sliab Fuait,' said Fergus; 'the three sons of Fiachna are these, after the Bull; that is, Rus and Dairi and Imchath,' said Fergus.

'Another company has come there to the hill, to Slemon Midi,' said Mac Roth. 'A man lively, fiery, before it; eyes very red, of a champion, in his head; a many-coloured cloak about him; a chain of silver thereon; a grey shield on his left; [a sword] with a hilt of silver at his side; a spear, excellent with a striking of cruelty in his vengeful right hand; a shirt white, hooded, to his knee. A company very red, with wounds, about him, and he himself wounded and bleeding.'

'That,' said Fergus, 'is the bold one, unsparing; that is the tearing; it is the boar [Note: Ir. *rop*, said to be a beast that wounds or gores.] of combat, it is the mad bull; it is the victorious one of Baile; it is the warlike one of the gap; it is the champion of Colptha, the door of war of the north of Ireland: that is, Menn Mac Salchalca from Corann. To avenge his wounds upon you has that man come,' said Fergus.

'Another company has come there to the hill, to Slemon Midi,' said Mac Roth, 'and they very heroic, mutually willing. A warrior grey, great, broad, tall, before it. Hair dark, curly, on him; a cloak red, woollen, about him; a shirt excellent; a brooch of gold over his arms in his cloak; a sword, excellent, with hilt of white silver on his left; a red shield has he; a spear-head broad-grey on a fair shaft [Note: Conjecture; the Irish is obscure.] of ash in his hand.

'A man of three strong blows who has so come,' said Fergus; 'a man of three roads, a man of three highways, a man of three gifts, a man of three shouts, who breaks battles on enemies in another province: Fergrae Mac Findchoime from Corann is that.'

'Another company has come there to the hill, to Slemon Midi,' said Mac Roth. 'Its appearance is greater than a cantred. A warrior white-breasted, very fair, before it; like to Ailill yonder in size and beauty and equipment and raiment. A crown of gold above his head; a cloak excellent folded about him; a brooch of gold in the cloak on his breast; a shirt with red ornamentation round about him; a shield wound-giving with rims of gold; the pillar of a palace in his hand; a sword gold-hilted on his shoulders.'

'It is a sea over rivers who has so come, truly,' said Fergus; 'it is a fierce glow of fire; his rage towards foes is insupportable: Furbaidi Ferbend is that,' said Fergus.

'Another company has come there to the hill, to Slemon Midi,' said Mac Roth. 'Very heroic, innumerable,' said Mac Roth; 'strange garments, various, about them, different from other companies. Famously have they come, both in arms and raiment and dress. A great host and fierce is that company. A lad flame red before it; the most beautiful of the forms of men his form; ... a shield with white boss in his hand, the shield of gold and a rim of gold round it; a spear sharp, light, with in his hand; a cloak purple, fringed, folded about him; a brooch of silver in the cloak, on his breast; a shirt white, hooded, with red ornamentation, about him; a sword gold-hilted over his dress outside.'

Therewith Fergus is silent.

'I do not know indeed,' said Fergus, 'the like of this lad in Ulster, except that I think it is the men of Temair about a lad proper, wonderful, noble: with Erc, son of Coirpre Niafer and of Conchobar's daughter. They love not one another; ---- without his father's leave has that man come, to help his grandfather. It is through the combat of that lad,' said Fergus, 'that you will be defeated in the battle. That lad knows not terror nor fear at coming to you among them into the midst of your battalion. It would be like men that the warriors of the men of Ulster will roar in saving the calf their heart, in striking the battle. There will come to them a feeling of kinship at seeing that lad in the great battle, striking the battle before them. There will be heard the rumble of Conchobar's sword like the barking of a watch-dog in saving the lad. He will throw three walls of men about the battle in seeking the lad. It will be with the affection of kinsmen that the warriors of Ulster will attack the countless host,' said Fergus.

'I think it long,' said Mac Roth, 'to be recounting all that I have seen, but I have come meanwhile (?) with tidings to you.'

'You have brought it,' said Fergus.

'Conall Cernach has not come with his great company,' said Mac Roth; 'the three sons of Conchobar with their three cantreds have not come; Cuchulainn too has not come there after his wounding in combat against odds. Unless it is a warrior with one chariot,' said Mac Roth, 'I think it would be he who has come there. Two horses ... under his chariot; they are long-tailed, broad-hoofed, broad above, narrow beneath, high-headed, great of curve, thin-mouthed, with distended nostrils. Two wheels black, ----, with tyres even, smooth-running; the body very high, clattering; the tent ... therein; the pillars carved. The warrior in that chariot four-square, purple-faced; hair cropped short on the top, curly, very black has he, down to his shoulders; ... a cloak red about him; four thirties of feat-poles (?) in each of his two arms. A sword gold-hilted on his left; shield and spear has he, and twenty-four javelins about him on strings and thongs. The charioteer in front of him; the back of the charioteer's head towards the horses, the reins grasped by his toes (?) before him; the chessboard spread between them, half the men of yellow gold, the others of white metal; the **buanfach** [Note: the name of a game; probably in the nature of chess or draughts.] under their thighs. Nine feats were performed by him on high.'

'Who is that, O Fergus?' said Ailill.

'An easy question,' said Fergus. 'Cuchulainn Mac Sualtaim from the *Sid*, [Note: Cuchulainn was of fairy birth.] and Loeg Mac Riangabra his charioteer. Cuchulainn is that,' said Fergus.

'Many hundreds and thousands,' said Mac Roth, 'have reached the camp of Ulster. Many heroes and champions and fighting-men have come with a race to the assembly. Many companies,' said Mac Roth, 'were reaching the same camp, of those who had not reached or come to the camp when I came; only,' said Mac Roth, 'my eye did not rest on hill or height of all that my eye reached from Fer Diad's Ford to Slemon Midi, but upon horse and man.'

'You saw the household of a man truly,' said Fergus.

Then Conchobar went with his hosts and took camp near the others. Conchobar asked for a truce till sunrise on the morrow from Ailill, and Ailill ratified it for the men of Ireland and for the exiles, and Conchobar ratified it for the Ulstermen; and then Conchobar's tents are pitched. The ground between them is a space, ----, bare, and the Ulstermen came to it before sunset. Then said the Morrigan in the twilight between the two camps: [Note: Rhetoric, seven lines]

Now Cuchulainn was at Fedan Chollna near them. Food was brought to him by the hospitallers that night; and they used to come to speak to him by day.

He did not kill any of them to the left of Fer Diad's Ford.

'Here is a small herd from the camp from the west to the camp to the east,' said the charioteer to Cuchulainn. 'Here is a troop of lads to meet them.'

'Those lads shall come,' said Cuchulainn. 'The little herd shall come over the plain. He who will not ---- (?) shall come to help the lads.'

This was done then as Cuchulainn had said.

'How do the lads of Ulster fight the battle?'

'Like men,' said the charioteer.

'It would be a vow for them, to fall in rescuing their herds,' said Cuchulainn. 'And now?'

'The beardless striplings are fighting now,' said the charioteer.

'Has a bright cloud come over the sun yet?'

'Not so,' said the charioteer.

'Alas, that I had not strength to go to them!' said Cuchulainn.

'There will be contest without that to-day,' said the charioteer, 'at sunrise; haughty folk fight the battle now,' said the charioteer, 'save that there are not kings there, for they are still asleep.'

Then Fachna said when the sun rose (or it is Conchobar who sang in his sleep):

'Arise, Kings of Macha, of mighty deeds, noble household, grind your weapons, fight the battle,' etc.

'Who has sung this?' said every one.

'Conchobar Mac Nessa,' said they; 'or Fachtna sang it,' said they. 'Sleep, sleep, save your sentinels.'

Loegaire the Victorious was heard: 'Arise, Kings of Macha,' etc.

'Who has sung that?' said every one.

'Loegaire the Victorious, son of Connad Buide Mac Ilech. Sleep, sleep, except your sentinels.'

'Wait for it still,' said Conchobar, 'till sunrise ... in the glens and heights of Ireland.'

When Cuchulainn saw the kings from the east taking their crowns on their heads and marshalling (?) the companies, Cuchulainn said to his charioteer that he should awaken the Ulstermen; and the charioteer said (or it is Amairgen, son of Eccet the poet, who said):

'Arise, Kings of Macha,' etc.

'I have awakened them,' said the charioteer. 'Thus have they come to the battle, quite naked, except for their arms only. He, the door of whose tent is east, has come out through it west.'

'It is a "goodly help of necessity,"' said Cuchulainn.

The adventures of the Ulstermen are not followed up here now. As for the men of Ireland, Badb and Net's wife and Nemain [Note: Nemain was the wife of Net, the war-god, according to Cormac.] called upon them that night on Garach and Irgarach, so that a hundred warriors of them died for terror; that was not the most peaceful of nights for them.

THE MUSTER OF THE MEN OF IRELAND HERE

Ailill Mac Matae sang that night before the battle, and said: 'Arise, arise,' etc [Note: Here follows a list of names.]

As for Cuchulainn, this is what is told here now.

'Look for us, O my friend, O Loeg, how the Ulstermen are fighting the battle now.'

'Like men,' said the charioteer.

'Though I were to go with my chariot, and Oen the charioteer of Conall Cernach with his chariot, so that we should go from one wing to the other along the dense mass, neither hoofs nor tyres shall go through it.'

'That is the stuff for a great battle,' said Cuchulainn. 'Nothing must be done in the battle,' said Cuchulainn to his charioteer, 'that we shall not know from you.'

'That will be true, so far as I can,' said the charioteer. 'The place where the warriors are now from the west,' said the charioteer, 'they make a breach in the battle eastwards. Their first defence from the east, they make a breach in the battle westwards.'

'Alas! that I am not whole!' said Cuchulainn; 'my breach would be manifest like the rest.'

Then came the men of the bodyguard to the ford of the hosting. Fine the way in which the fightingmen came to the battle on Garach and Irgarach. Then came the nine chariot-men of the champions of Iruath, three before them on foot. Not more slowly did they come than the chariot-men. Medb did not let them into the battle, for dragging Ailill out of the battle if it is him they should defeat, or for killing Conchobar if it is he who should be defeated.

Then his charioteer told Cuchulainn that Ailill and Medb were asking Fergus to go into the battle; and they said to him that it was only right for him to do it, for they had done him much kindness on his exile.

'If I had my sword indeed,' said Fergus, 'the heads of men over shields would be more numerous with me than hailstones in the mire to which come the horses of a king after they have broken into the land (?).'

Then Fergus made this oath: 'I swear, etc., there would be broken by me cheeks of men from their necks, necks of men with their (lower) arms, arms of men with their elbows, elbows of men with their arms, arms of men with their fists, fists of men with their fingers, fingers of men with their nails, [nails] of men with their skull-roofs, skull-roofs of men with their middle, middle of men with their thighs, thighs of men with their knees, knees of men with their calves, calves of men with their feet, feet of men with their toes, toes of men with their nails. I would make their necks whizz (?) ---- as a bee would move to and fro on a day of beauty (?).'

Then Ailill said to his charioteer: 'Let there come to me the sword which destroys skin. I swear by the god by whom my people swear, if you have its bloom worse to-day than on the day on which I gave it to you in the hillside in the boundary of Ulster, though the men of Ireland were protecting you from me, they should not protect you.'

Then his sword was brought to Fergus, and Ailill said: 'Take thy sword,' etc. [Note: Rhetoric, twelve lines.]

'A pity for thee to fall on the field of battle, thick [with slain ?],' said Fergus to Ailill.

The Badb and Net's wife and the Nemain called on them that night on Garach and Irgarach; so that a hundred warriors of them died for terror. That was not the quietest of nights for them.

Then Fergus takes his arms and turns into the battle, and clears a gap of a hundred in the battle with his sword in his two hands. Then Medb took the arms of Fergus (?) and rushed into the battle, and she was victorious thrice, so that she was driven back by force of arms.

'I do not know,' said Conchobar to his retinue who were round him, 'before whom has the battle been broken against us from the north. Do you maintain the fight here, that I may go against him.'

'We will hold the place in which we are,' said the warriors, 'unless the earth bursts beneath us, or the heaven upon us from above, so that we shall break therefrom.'

Then Conchobar came against Fergus. He lifts his shield against him, i.e. Conchobar's shield Ochan, with three horns of gold on it, and four ----- of gold over it. Fergus strikes three blows on it, so that even the rim of his shield over his head did not touch him.

'Who of the Ulstermen holds the shield?' said Fergus.

'A man who is better than you,' said Conchobar; 'and he has brought you into exile into the dwellings of wolves and foxes, and he will repel you to-day in combat in the presence of the men of Ireland.'

Fergus aimed on him a blow of vengeance with his two hands on Conchobar, so that the point of the sword touched the ground behind him.

Cormac Condlongas put his hands upon him, and closed his two hands about his arm.

'----, O my friend, O Fergus,' said Cormac. '... Hostile is the friendship; right is your enmity; your compact has been destroyed; evil are the blows that you strike, O friend, O Fergus,' said Cormac.

'Whom shall I smite?' said Fergus.

'Smite the three hills ... in some other direction over them; turn your hand; smite about you on every side, and have no consideration for them. Take thought for the honour of Ulster: what has not been lost shall not be lost, if it be not lost through you to-day (?).'

'Go in some other direction, O Conchobar,' said Cormac to his father; 'this man will not put out his rage on the Ulstermen any more here.'

Fergus turned away. He slew a hundred warriors of Ulster in the first combat with the sword. He met Conall Cernach.

'Too great rage is that,' said Conall Cernach, 'on people and race, for a wanton.'

'What shall I do, O warriors?' said he.

'Smite the hills across them and the champions (?) round them,' said Conall Cernach.

Fergus smote the hills then, so that he struck the three Maela [Note: i.e. flat-topped hills.] of Meath with his three blows. Cuchulainn heard the blows then that Fergus gave on the hills or on the shield of Conchobar himself.

'Who strikes the three strong blows, great and distant?' said Cuchulainn.

... Then Loeg answered and said: 'The choice of men, Fergus Mac Roich the very bold, smites them.' ...

Then Cuchulainn said: 'Unloose quickly the hazeltwigs; blood covers men, play of swords will be made, men will be spent therefrom.'

Then his dry wisps spring from him on high, as far as ---- goes; and his hazel-twigs spring off, till they were in Mag Tuag in Connaught ... and he smote the head of each of the two handmaidens against the other, so that each of them was grey from the brain of the other. They came from Medb for pretended lamentation over him, that his wounds might burst forth on him; and to say that the Ulstermen had been defeated, and that Fergus had fallen in opposing the battle, since Cuchulainn's coming into the battle had been prevented. The contortion came on him, and twenty-seven skin-tunics were given to him, that used to be about him under strings and thongs when he went into battle; and he takes his chariot on his back with its body and its two tyres, and he made for Fergus round about the battle.

'Turn hither, O friend Fergus,' said Cuchulainn; and he did not answer till the third time. 'I swear by the god by whom the Ulstermen swear,' said he, 'I will wash thee as foam [Note: Reading with L.L.] (?) is washed in a pool, I will go over thee as the tail goes over a cat, I will smite thee as a fond mother smites her son.'

'Which of the men of Ireland speaks thus to me?' said Fergus.

'Cuchulainn Mac Sualtaim, sister's son to Conchobar,' said Cuchulainn; 'and avoid me,' said he.

'I have promised even that,' said Fergus.

'Your promise falls due, then,' said Cuchulainn.

'Good,' said Fergus, '(you avoided me), when you are pierced with wounds.'

Then Fergus went away with his cantred; the Leinstermen go and the Munstermen; and they left in the battle nine cantreds of Medb's and Ailill's and their seven sons.

In the middle of the day it is that Cuchulainn came into the battle; when the sun came into the leaves of the wood, it is then that he defeated the last company, so that there remained of the chariot only a handful of the ribs about the body, and a handful of the shafts about the wheel.

Cuchulainn overtook Medb then when he went into the battle.

'Protect me,' said Medb.

'Though I should slay thee with a slaying, it were lawful for me,' said Cuchulainn.

Then he protected her, because he used not to slay women. He convoyed them westward, till they passed Ath Luain. Then he stopped. He struck three blows with his sword on the stone in Ath Luain. Their name is the Maelana [Note: i.e., flat-topped hills] of Ath Luain.

When the battle was broken, then said Medb to Fergus: 'Faults and meet here to-day, O Fergus,' said she.

'It is customary,' said Fergus, 'to every herd which a mare precedes; ... after a woman who has ill consulted their interest.'

They take away the Bull then in that morning of the battle, so that he met the White-horned at Tarbga in Mag Ai; i.e. Tarbguba or Tarbgleo.[Note: 'Bull-Sorrow or Bull-Fight,' etymological explanation of Tarbga.] The first name of that hill was Roi Dedond. Every one who escaped in the fight was intent on nothing but beholding the two Bulls fighting.

Bricriu Poison-tongue was in the west in his sadness after Fergus had broken his head with his draughtmen [Note: This story is told in the **Echtra Nerai**. (See **Revue Celtique**, vol. x. p. 227.)] He came with the rest then to see the combat of the Bulls. The two Bulls went in fighting over Bricriu, so that he died therefrom. That is the Death of Bricriu.

The foot of the Dun of Cualnge lighted on the horn of the other. For a day and a night he did not draw his foot towards him, till Fergus incited him and plied a rod along his body.

''Twere no good luck,' said Fergus, 'that this conbative old calf which has been brought here should leave the honour of clan and race; and on both sides men have been left dead through you.' Therewith he drew his foot to him so that his leg (?) was broken, and the horn sprang from the other and was in the mountain by him. It was Sliab n-Adarca [Note: Mountain of the Horn.] afterwards.

He carried them then a journey of a day and a night, till he lighted in the loch which is by Cruachan, and he came to Cruachan out of it with the loin and the shoulder-blade and the liver of the other on his horns. Then the hosts came to kill him. Fergus did not allow it, but that he should go where he pleased. He came then to his land and drank a draught in Findlethe on coming. It is there that he left the shoulderblade of the other. Findlethe afterwards was the name of the land. He drank another draught in Ath Luain; he left the loin of the other there: hence is Ath Luain. He gave forth his roar on Iraird Chuillend; it was heard through all the province. He drank a draught in Tromma. There the liver of the other fell from his horns; hence is Tromma. He came to Etan Tairb. [Note: The Bull's Forehead.] He put his forehead against the hill at Ath Da Ferta; hence is Etan Tairb in Mag Murthemne. Then he went on the road of Midluachair in Cuib. There he used to be with the milkless cow of Dairi, and he made a trench there. Hence is Gort Buraig. [Note: The Field of the Trench.] Then he went till he died between Ulster and Iveagh at Druim Tairb. Druim Tairb is the name of that place.

Ailill and Medb made peace with the Ulstermen and with Cuchulainn. For seven years after there was no wounding of men between them. Findabair stayed with Cuchulainn, and the Connaughtmen went to their country, and the Ulstermen to Emain Macha with their great triumph. Finit, amen.

The Codes Of Hammurabi And Moses
W. W. Davies

QTY

The discovery of the Hammurabi Code is one of the greatest achievements of archaeology, and is of paramount interest, not only to the student of the Bible, but also to all those interested in ancient history...

Religion　**ISBN:** *1-59462-338-4*　　**Pages:**132
MSRP $12.95

The Theory of Moral Sentiments
Adam Smith

QTY

This work from 1749. contains original theories of conscience amd moral judgment and it is the foundation for systemof morals.

Philosophy　**ISBN:** *1-59462-777-0*　　**Pages:**536
MSRP $19.95

Jessica's First Prayer
Hesba Stretton

QTY

In a screened and secluded corner of one of the many railway-bridges which span the streets of London there could be seen a few years ago, from five o'clock every morning until half past eight, a tidily set-out coffee-stall, consisting of a trestle and board, upon which stood two large tin cans, with a small fire of charcoal burning under each so as to keep the coffee boiling during the early hours of the morning when the work-people were thronging into the city on their way to their daily toil...

Pages:84

Childrens　**ISBN:** *1-59462-373-2*　　*MSRP $9.95*

My Life and Work
Henry Ford

QTY

Henry Ford revolutionized the world with his implementation of mass production for the Model T automobile. Gain valuable business insight into his life and work with his own auto-biography... "We have only started on our development of our country we have not as yet, with all our talk of wonderful progress, done more than scratch the surface. The progress has been wonderful enough but..."

Pages:300

Biographies/　**ISBN:** *1-59462-198-5*　　*MSRP $21.95*

The Art of Cross-Examination
Francis Wellman

QTY

I presume it is the experience of every author, after his first book is published upon an important subject, to be almost overwhelmed with a wealth of ideas and illustrations which could readily have been included in his book, and which to his own mind, at least, seem to make a second edition inevitable. Such certainly was the case with me; and when the first edition had reached its sixth impression in five months, I rejoiced to learn that it seemed to my publishers that the book had met with a sufficiently favorable reception to justify a second and considerably enlarged edition. ...

Pages:412

Reference   ISBN: *1-59462-647-2*   *MSRP $19.95*

On the Duty of Civil Disobedience
Henry David Thoreau

QTY

Thoreau wrote his famous essay, On the Duty of Civil Disobedience, as a protest against an unjust but popular war and the immoral but popular institution of slave-owning. He did more than write—he declined to pay his taxes, and was hauled off to gaol in consequence. Who can say how much this refusal of his hastened the end of the war and of slavery ?

Law   ISBN: *1-59462-747-9*   **Pages:48**

MSRP $7.45

Dream Psychology Psychoanalysis for Beginners
Sigmund Freud

QTY

Sigmund Freud, born Sigismund Schlomo Freud (May 6, 1856 - September 23, 1939), was a Jewish-Austrian neurologist and psychiatrist who co-founded the psychoanalytic school of psychology. Freud is best known for his theories of the unconscious mind, especially involving the mechanism of repression; his redefinition of sexual desire as mobile and directed towards a wide variety of objects; and his therapeutic techniques, especially his understanding of transference in the therapeutic relationship and the presumed value of dreams as sources of insight into unconscious desires.

Pages:196

Psychology   ISBN: *1-59462-905-6*   *MSRP $15.45*

The Miracle of Right Thought
Orison Swett Marden

QTY

Believe with all of your heart that you will do what you were made to do. When the mind has once formed the habit of holding cheerful, happy, prosperous pictures, it will not be easy to form the opposite habit. It does not matter how improbable or how far away this realization may see, or how dark the prospects may be, if we visualize them as best we can, as vividly as possible, hold tenaciously to them and vigorously struggle to attain them, they will gradually become actualized, realized in the life. But a desire, a longing without endeavor, a yearning abandoned or held indifferently will vanish without realization.

Pages:360

Self Help   ISBN: *1-59462-644-8*   *MSRP $25.45*

www.bookjungle.com *email: sales@bookjungle.com fax: 630-214-0564 mail: Book Jungle PO Box 2226 Champaign, IL 61825*

QTY

The Rosicrucian Cosmo-Conception Mystic Christianity *by Max Heindel*　ISBN: *1-59462-188-8*　**$38.95**
The Rosicrucian Cosmo-conception is not dogmatic, neither does it appeal to any other authority than the reason of the student. It is: not controversial, but is: sent forth in the, hope that it may help to clear...　New Age/Religion Pages 646

Abandonment To Divine Providence *by Jean-Pierre de Caussade*　ISBN: *1-59462-228-0*　**$25.95**
"The Rev. Jean Pierre de Caussade was one of the most remarkable spiritual writers of the Society of Jesus in France in the 18th Century. His death took place at Toulouse in 1751. His works have gone through many editions and have been republished...　Inspirational/Religion Pages 400

Mental Chemistry *by Charles Haanel*　ISBN: *1-59462-192-6*　**$23.95**
Mental Chemistry allows the change of material conditions by combining and appropriately utilizing the power of the mind. Much like applied chemistry creates something new and unique out of careful combinations of chemicals the mastery of mental chemistry...　New Age Pages 354

The Letters of Robert Browning and Elizabeth Barret Barrett 1845-1846 vol II　ISBN: *1-59462-193-4*　**$35.95**
by Robert Browning and Elizabeth Barrett　Biographies Pages 596

Gleanings In Genesis (volume I) *by Arthur W. Pink*　ISBN: *1-59462-130-6*　**$27.45**
Appropriately has Genesis been termed "the seed plot of the Bible" for in it we have, in germ form, almost all of the great doctrines which are afterwards fully developed in the books of Scripture which follow...　Religion/Inspirational Pages 420

The Master Key *by L. W. de Laurence*　ISBN: *1-59462-001-6*　**$30.95**
In no branch of human knowledge has there been a more lively increase of the spirit of research during the past few years than in the study of Psychology, Concentration and Mental Discipline. The requests for authentic lessons in Thought Control, Mental Discipline and...　New Age/Business Pages 422

The Lesser Key Of Solomon Goetia *by L. W. de Laurence*　ISBN: *1-59462-092-X*　**$9.95**
This translation of the first book of the "Lernegton" which is now for the first time made accessible to students of Talismanic Magic was done, after careful collation and edition, from numerous Ancient Manuscripts in Hebrew, Latin, and French...　New Age/Occult Pages 92

Rubaiyat Of Omar Khayyam *by Edward Fitzgerald*　ISBN:*1-59462-332-5*　**$13.95**
Edward Fitzgerald, whom the world has already learned, in spite of his own efforts to remain within the shadow of anonymity, to look upon as one of the rarest poets of the century, was born at Bredfield, in Suffolk, on the 31st of March, 1809. He was the third son of John Purcell...　Music Pages 172

Ancient Law *by Henry Maine*　ISBN: *1-59462-128-4*　**$29.95**
The chief object of the following pages is to indicate some of the earliest ideas of mankind, as they are reflected in Ancient Law, and to point out the relation of those ideas to modern thought.　Religiom/History Pages 452

Far-Away Stories *by William J. Locke*　ISBN: *1-59462-129-2*　**$19.45**
"Good wine needs no bush, but a collection of mixed vintages does. And this book is just such a collection. Some of the stories I do not want to remain buried for ever in the museum files of dead magazine-numbers an author's not unpardonable vanity..."　Fiction Pages 272

Life of David Crockett *by David Crockett*　ISBN: *1-59462-250-7*　**$27.45**
"Colonel David Crockett was one of the most remarkable men of the times in which he lived. Born in humble life, but gifted with a strong will, an indomitable courage, and unremitting perseverance...　Biographies/New Age Pages 424

Lip-Reading *by Edward Nitchie*　ISBN: *1-59462-206-X*　**$25.95**
Edward B. Nitchie, founder of the New York School for the Hard of Hearing, now the Nitchie School of Lip-Reading, Inc, wrote "LIP-READING Principles and Practice". The development and perfecting of this meritorious work on lip-reading was an undertaking...　How-to Pages 400

A Handbook of Suggestive Therapeutics, Applied Hypnotism, Psychic Science　ISBN: *1-59462-214-0*　**$24.95**
by Henry Munro　Health/New Age/Health/Self-help Pages 376

A Doll's House: and Two Other Plays *by Henrik Ibsen*　ISBN: *1-59462-112-8*　**$19.95**
Henrik Ibsen created this classic when in revolutionary 1848 Rome. Introducing some striking concepts in playwriting for the realist genre, this play has been studied the world over.　Fiction/Classics/Plays 308

The Light of Asia *by sir Edwin Arnold*　ISBN: *1-59462-204-3*　**$13.95**
In this poetic masterpiece, Edwin Arnold describes the life and teachings of Buddha. The man who was to become known as Buddha to the world was born as Prince Gautama of India but he rejected the worldly riches and abandoned the reigns of power when...　Religion/History/Biographies Pages 170

The Complete Works of Guy de Maupassant *by Guy de Maupassant*　ISBN: *1-59462-157-8*　**$16.95**
"For days and days, nights and nights, I had dreamed of that first kiss which was to consecrate our engagement, and I knew not on what spot I should put my lips..."　Fiction/Classics Pages 240

The Art of Cross-Examination *by Francis L. Wellman*　ISBN: *1-59462-309-0*　**$26.95**
Written by a renowned trial lawyer, Wellman imparts his experience and uses case studies to explain how to use psychology to extract desired information through questioning.　How-to/Science/Reference Pages 408

Answered or Unanswered? *by Louisa Vaughan*　ISBN: *1-59462-248-5*　**$10.95**
Miracles of Faith in China　Religion Pages 112

The Edinburgh Lectures on Mental Science (1909) *by Thomas*　ISBN: *1-59462-008-3*　**$11.95**
This book contains the substance of a course of lectures recently given by the writer in the Queen Street Hail, Edinburgh. Its purpose is to indicate the Natural Principles governing the relation between Mental Action and Material Conditions...　New Age/Psychology Pages 148

Ayesha *by H. Rider Haggard*　ISBN: *1-59462-301-5*　**$24.95**
Verily and indeed it is the unexpected that happens! Probably if there was one person upon the earth from whom the Editor of this, and of a certain previous history, did not expect to hear again...　Classics Pages 380

Ayala's Angel *by Anthony Trollope*　ISBN: *1-59462-352-X*　**$29.95**
The two girls were both pretty, but Lucy who was twenty-one who supposed to be simple and comparatively unattractive, whereas Ayala was credited, as her Bombwhat romantic name might show, with poetic charm and a taste for romance. Ayala when her father died was nineteen...　Fiction Pages 484

The American Commonwealth *by James Bryce*　ISBN: *1-59462-286-8*　**$34.45**
An interpretation of American democratic political theory. It examines political mechanics and society from the perspective of Scotsman James Bryce　Politics Pages 572

Stories of the Pilgrims *by Margaret P. Pumphrey*　ISBN: *1-59462-116-0*　**$17.95**
This book explores pilgrims religious oppression in England as well as their escape to Holland and eventual crossing to America on the Mayflower, and their early days in New England...　History Pages 268

www.bookjungle.com *email: sales@bookjungle.com fax: 630-214-0564 mail: Book Jungle PO Box 2226 Champaign, IL 61825*

QTY

The Fasting Cure *by Sinclair Upton*   ISBN: *1-59462-222-1*   **$13.95**
In the Cosmopolitan Magazine for May, 1910, and in the Contemporary Review (London) for April, 1910, I published an article dealing with my experiences in fasting. I have written a great many magazine articles, but never one which attracted so much attention... New Age/Self Help/Health Pages 164

Hebrew Astrology *by Sepharial*   ISBN: *1-59462-308-2*   **$13.45**
In these days of advanced thinking it is a matter of common observation that we have left many of the old landmarks behind and that we are now pressing forward to greater heights and to a wider horizon than that which represented the mind-content of our progenitors... Astrology Pages 144

Thought Vibration or The Law of Attraction in the Thought World   ISBN: *1-59462-127-6*   **$12.95**

by William Walker Atkinson   Psychology/Religion Pages 144

Optimism *by Helen Keller*   ISBN: *1-59462-108-X*   **$15.95**
Helen Keller was blind, deaf, and mute since 19 months old, yet famously learned how to overcome these handicaps, communicate with the world, and spread her lectures promoting optimism. An inspiring read for everyone... Biographies/Inspirational Pages 84

Sara Crewe *by Frances Burnett*   ISBN: *1-59462-360-0*   **$9.45**
In the first place, Miss Minchin lived in London. Her home was a large, dull, tall one, in a large, dull square, where all the houses were alike, and all the sparrows were alike, and where all the door-knockers made the same heavy sound... Childrens/Classic Pages 88

The Autobiography of Benjamin Franklin *by Benjamin Franklin*   ISBN: *1-59462-135-7*   **$24.95**
The Autobiography of Benjamin Franklin has probably been more extensively read than any other American historical work, and no other book of its kind has had such ups and downs of fortune. Franklin lived for many years in England, where he was agent... Biographies/History Pages 332

Name	
Email	
Telephone	
Address	
City, State ZIP	

☐ **Credit Card**   ☐ **Check / Money Order**

Credit Card Number	
Expiration Date	
Signature	

Please Mail to: Book Jungle
PO Box 2226
Champaign, IL 61825
or Fax to: 630-214-0564

ORDERING INFORMATION

web*: www.bookjungle.com*
email*: sales@bookjungle.com*
fax*: 630-214-0564*
mail*: Book Jungle PO Box 2226 Champaign, IL 61825*
or PayPal *to sales@bookjungle.com*

Please contact us for bulk discounts

DIRECT-ORDER TERMS

**20% Discount if You Order
Two or More Books**
Free Domestic Shipping!
Accepted: Master Card, Visa,
Discover, American Express